FOR THE SAKE OF MY

Engineering Guitaring Optimism

Ajay Setia

Harleen Walia

POWER PUBLISHERS
www.power-publishers.com

Copyright: **Ajay Setia**

Published by: Power Publishers,
www.Power-Publishers.com
Swabhumi Residency,
P-12 Motijheel Avenue,
Block 2, 1st floor,
Kolkata 700074.

Composing & Printing: JÑANALOK Infotech
www.jnanalok-books.com
24 Baghajatin Road
Kolkata - 700036

Cover Design: Tisha Mukherjee

First Published: April 2013

ISBN number: 978-93-82792-68-0

Price: ₹ 200/-

Available from: www.purushottam-publishers.com
www.Power-Publishers.com
www.infibeam.com
www.crossword.in
www.Flipkart.com
www.uRead.com

Vote of Thanks

First the real good ones!

I thank Harleen Walia, the girl who has beautified my simple words and gave my thoughts a horizon that could form story. And for keeping cool at all the times I get mad.

I would thank mom & dad for being an unmoved support and blessing me with their trust at every moment that passes us by. God for giving me experiences that I loved being a part of, the best amongst which is this book. Life without you people would have meant deficient.

Acknowledgements are not always about the brighter side. I have list too long to name here of people, who have cut me down for ever. Though, all those bitter things hardly made a difference, but they do form a part of my first book. But all those out there, please don't devalue our efforts by taking this as my answer.

Ajay Setia

This is the part that I eagerly awaited to write!

My first thanks would go to the invisible man in the boundless sky for writing wonderful stories an insignificant fraction of which we sometimes put down in black and white. I would thank my family for tolerating me and treating me better than I deserve every time.

My fate for being that nice to me and making my dream of this book come true. I thank my friends who make life look worthwhile.

And most importantly, someone who made everything possible, Ajay Setia. No matter what he claims, I believe he was just too sweet to make me write this. Yes despite all those clashes, it's been real pleasure writing with him. His presence saved me from the headache of worrying about my nonsensical writing. 'Thanks' is too small a word for my biggest critic and best supporter in one soul. Just wanted to say, nothing would have been possible without you around.

Harleen Walia

Prologue

There has never been a day more awaited for me than this one. Though I had longed for this, but reaching where I stand today has meant leaving infinite things I owned. I can't help but believing. Heading towards the place I have never been before, the past is pulling but I have to look forward and try to figure out my future. A new life, though it is miles away, waits.

Though I had never imagined it could happen, but amidst of thousands of people at Delhi Airport. I feel missing. Through the glass pane, I see people landing and being welcomed by their families, their loved ones. The sight is fruitful indeed.

But this is just not the place, where people accumulate, looking forward to destinations. Rather, it is where uncountable loved ones are forced to part from each other. Ample of thoughts I brush away before nostalgia takes over me, and find something to do other than anticipating. Having submitted my luggage to the luggage counter, I have nothing much in hand, except the bag which carries the things I can never travel without. And something more important!

I pull out my cherished possession as I lie back waiting on the chair & begin to write in it about my day so far. Airport shopping, a variety of nationalities, reunited smiles, heart-shattering partitions, I have so much to write about, but writing in crowd has never been a pleasant experience for me. But done enough with spotting every possible variety of the crowd & wandering in the place for reunions & good-byes, I make attempts to portray the cobwebs my mind is caught in to. With less than three lines I write, I give up the idea and close it down.

Attempts to indulge myself in the surroundings fail another time. There's no way possible for me to spend the delayed hours of my flight staring at foreigners with blue hair, and couples with blushing smiles. Immersed in the world of thoughts, I lay my eyes on its front cover. As I flip through its pages, the calendar catches my attention, as I find the date- 28th march 2012 encircled and 'Only till' written over it. It is today's date. But I recollect that it was marked 7 months back. Back then, I had no clue that reaching this date would need me to get through so many ravels.

I have not read it since a long back, and the thought of reading is tempting. It encloses memoirs of the past that I could not let it slip through my fingers. Had always been paranoid about being cheery, I'm sure that the last I want is to feel more nostalgic. A million thoughts cloud my mind and I shuttle back & forth. Finally, I make up my mind and open up the pages on which I have bared my heart from ages. It transports me not to the moment when the mark was drawn, but to a long way back.

I have left that place years back, and those people, some of them still occupy a place in my life, a few others, a corner in my heart, that I can never take back. I wonder sometimes if I miss something, Sometimes, I smile back to the question, and sometimes I laugh it out. But most of the time, I tend to ignore it. But the real answer and all that I want to say is.

The First Light

29th September 2007

"Hello..."

"Where, the hell, have you reached man?" Pulkit said, as he cut me off in the rudest tone his vocal cords were capable of producing. Not that it's the way he talks. In fact, it was quite in contrast to his simple peaceful demeanor. He hardly ever lost his calm. But that morning, his voice was pouring furiousness. Something that I had not witnessed in him since the day we became friends with each other.

I had met Pulkit almost in the 2nd week of the college and the very 1st interaction told me that he was an odd one out in a class of amazing snobs.

"I'm just on the way, dude. Just reached!" I said, trying to pacify his anger.

"That is exactly what you told me half an hour ago. I'm waiting for you like fools from past one hour." I removed the cell-phone from my ear and checked the time, as Pulkit continued to blow curses over me. My goodness, it was already 10 a.m.!!!!

I could hear his presumably high voice as I re-placed the phone. "No matter how fast you'll ride, we'll need another half an hour to travel down the 28 km-long stretch."

"Calm down, we won't." I said, looking at things messed up around me.

"Just tell me one thing. Are you coming to pick me up or should I find another way to reach at my fresher's party?"

"Buddy chill, don't worry. I'm right on the way. I'll pick you up in exactly 10 minutes. By the way, it is my fresher's too."

"Alright, no more than that."

"Yeah yeah, but for that I need to keep the phone & ride faster. See you. " I said & hung up the phone, not to ride but to change into my clothes.

The very moment Pulkit called, I had just stepped out of the bathroom & was yet to get ready. But, telling him my actual physical location would have meant like inviting him to hang me up with a rope to the fan rotating exactly above me.

In a nick of seconds, I wore my favourite white shirt, a pair of denims, and my new jacket which I had brought for the occasion. My fastest ever! I struggled with my hair as my mind imagined Pulkit getting mad with anger while it was almost 10: 25 a.m.

At times, when you almost beg time to run slower, your clock shoots up like a speedometer racing up & higher. I left home as I saw Pulkit's call again. Before I left, I made sure that I had picked up what I needed the most, the bag.

Pulkit was already standing outside his home, as I reached there. Putting on the charade of ire, Pulkit hardly acknowledged my emergence. But like always he could not help keeping himself off the mark of sarcasm, as he said that ironic 'Thank you'. On my end, I crossed my heart that it was really tough to recognize him from some distance.

Today what made me awestruck was his dressing. In that black shirt and denims, he looked better than ever. His glasses replaced by contacts, I mean, where was my nerdy best friend? But, he had painted a sore expression on his face. And those expressions could give complex to any pouting kid. Sad for him, they did nothing else than making me laugh. That's all I do, misplacing my laughter to raise other people's anguish all the time.

But, I dared not mess it up anymore for badly disappointed almost blood thirsty friend of mine. To control my muted laughter, I said, "Looking dashing, bro." But his expression clearly said that he was not in the mood to get entertained. He was infuriated as hell. I was thinking hard to find something to ease his silent grumble and help him improve that grave expression, when finally he uttered something rather than just staring me.

"May we please proceed now, or I suppose you have planned to spend the entire day right here??" He said.

"No no. I'm really very sorry. I'm."

"There you're. It's ok. Chuck it now." he said. I envy people who can chuck the disturbances so easily. But I'd warned you this is Pulkit. The calm, sensible and forgiving guy people silently ask for in their prayers.

"Let's go. By the way." I said.

"What does this huge bag carry?? Don't tell me we have to go somewhere else too now."

"We don't. And this is for youuuur fresher's party only. " I said, reflecting sarcasm in my voice.

"Oh, and it carries what??"

"A keyboard." I answered, waiting when his queries would end & we would start with the journey.

"Keyboard! What for?? Where are the monitor & processor, Mr. Potential computer engineer??" he said. It seemed like now it was his turn to put me on a patience test.

"Man, this is not the computer's keyboard. It's my musical keyboard!!!"

A week before the Fresher's Party, our seniors had turned up to invite us all. While many of my classmates frightened it as if they were man-eaters, I was keen about the interaction.

Nonetheless, I was thoroughly excited by the idea when they announced that aspirants for the Mr. & Ms. Fresher's tag could prepare mono-performances. And for me, playing keyboard was not any option, but the only choice. It was the only thing I remembered I had enjoyed the most till the journey that far.

"Keyboard?? Synthesizer!! Ever heard of a thing like that??"

"Of course, I must have been out of my mind to ask such a thing. But, it will be really difficult for you to hold it & ride thoroughly."

"It will be, but when did I say I'm the one holding it??" I shrugged.

He understood the mischief in my voice. "It means what??"

"Means you. Do hold the keyboard firmly." I smiled at him.

"No way. I'm just not carrying this."

"But why??"

"What do you mean by 'why'??

"I'm just not ruining the crease of my suit for holding this rack-sack of yours."

"Suit? Well placed concerns, Huh?" I said with the hint of sarcasm, as Pulkit rolled his eyes.

"Dude, do you realize I have left Tanya just because I could pick you up?? And you are calling my keyboard a rack-sack."

"You left Tanya?? You??" he was stunned by my last statement.

"Yes, may be if I would have offered her a lift, she would not have denied. But I preferred you over the girl I like. And that's how you pay me back??" I said blushing, and overjoyed in my heart of hearts dreaming something that had rare chances to come true.

"Ohoho. As if she is dying to sit on your bike?"

"Who knows she might be??" I said in an optimistic tone which 90 percent of Indian guys survive on. Pulkit almost realized there was hardly any point in rebelling any further.

"Fine. Give it to me, you keyboard lover." He sat on the bike as I pressed the clutch & started the bike. "Uhm, music lover precisely." I corrected him.

"Yeah, and get your Tanya to hold this on the way back. I'll travel by a bus." Pulkit said, teasing me.

I smiled wondering how conveniently we guys dragged a chick into our rifts, that too when she is immeasurably far-off in a totally another world. Tanya had become my 'crush', if that word was appropriate for what I felt for her. I still remember the 1st time I noticed her, while she was struggling with a program in the Computers lab. Not a surprise that she was so engrossed that she did not even notice me, working just next to her, who was engrossed in noticing her. Words like cute, pretty seem an understatement for girls like her. Fortunately, we got to talk when I helped her out by removing the error from the computer program.

From that very moment, I could not help looking at her & taking a glance whenever possible. She was completely worth it. In fact, much more. But after that, there was a rare chance that we could talk. She was always surrounded by her friends. And even when she was not, all I could manage to do was say a 'Hii' and run out of her sight. Many a time, her presence in the radius of 2 meters nerved me and made my heart pick up its rate.

Fortunately, we were not as late as Pulkit had assumed us to be at Hotel Saffron, known faces with unknown Avatars welcomed me. So much that I could write about my classmates out there, but in one line-. Make-up has the ability to change looks terrifically, and sometimes terribly. In the land of blondes, I was searching for that girl with dark hair whose images had been haunting me since the moment I entered the Party Hall. For Tanya! Magic spread across the hall, as I saw her in that red dress. She looked arresting. And the very second my glance fell upon her my heart went off to her. I would be the happiest man, if only I could tell her that. But even before I could manage to look at her properly, the seniors made a call.

Standing at the stage, I could almost see everyone present there. The beautifully decorated hall sent me sparks of enthusiasm. Bunches of tulip flowers interlaced the party hall of Hotel Saffron. Dim florescent lights, glinting after every couple of seconds, complimented the ambiance making it even perfect. Each one of us was being called up for the 'introduction' Round.

Most of the girls were looking pretty; some of them even drop dead gorgeous. But, no fraction of my imagination could make Tanya look better than she did that day. She was a piece of marvel. My eyes ran across the hall to find my sugared treat. I had seen her only twice from the moment I had come. Unable to spot her, my smile began to fade. But I had to keep up, as the announcers gave me a green signal to start my intro.

With words reflecting utmost courtesy to the seniors & my friends, I began my introduction. Eyes surely got widened when I lied a bit about my aggregate on 12th std., giving a boost of certain percents, some due to appreciation, of our seniors, while some because of disgust, of those who knew it was a hoax.

I announced about my fondness for music, the only icing on my sponge cake. How do I miss that? I spoke with utter confidence & fluency. Luckily, Google had given me enough catchy words. A number of practices, that I did last night in front of the mirror, bore fruits and I was promoted to the next round.

When the rest of my classmates were choosing what to perform in the performance round, unexpected consciousness was taking all over me. All of a sudden, carrying the keyboard seemed pretty odd over other simple idyllic options like singing or dancing.

It was undoubtedly an extra effort, I knew from the beginning, but I did not want anyone to infer it as an over-hype act.

"You look uncomfortable, what is wrong??" Pulkit said, as we stood at the backstage.

"Nothing, do you think keyboard will look like an exaggerated effort for a mere round?" Even if I try, I could not hide anything from him.

"Are you nuts?? It would not. People are performing. So are you. Nothing's wrong about that."

"But it would appear childish or may be a publicity stunt." I said, recklessly confused.

"As if you don't need publicity?? Do you know you are over-rating yourself??" he mocked.

"This is not the perfect time to make fun, man."

"Yeah. Don't make faces. You are just complicating damn simple things, give your silly mind some peace. Now, pick up your keyboard & go ahead. It'll go great." He said.

"Are you saying this because you really feel that or the reason behind is that you don't want your hard work of carrying the keyboard to go waste??" I teased him, as my name was announced.

"To be honest, the latter actually." He said, as we both laughed.

A keyboard is irresistibly pulling for my fingers, and how much I loved this fact, when I was up there for performing. I played two songs which expressed the elation & ecstasy of new college students, which instilled zeal among the audiences. And seeing them enjoy, my confidence soared up. The reaction that came by their side was much better than my expectations. The round of applause that followed after the 6-minute long performance made it evident to me that bringing a keyboard could not be a mistake. It was surely not. Many of my other classmates had done well at their turns. They were gifted either by talented voices or elastic bones.

In the 3rd round, the judgment panel was meant to put up questions to the finalists for Mr. & Ms. Fresher's tag.

"My question to you is 'What's your take on life'?" The only girl amongst the judges asked me, as I stood with 3 competitors of mine.

In hearts of my heart, I've had a blast the moment she completed her question, because I felt answer to her question was as easy as grabbing a candy from a 6year-old. I began thinking of an impressive answer, but almost the next moment, the announcer asked me to start answering.

I glanced at the judges, brought the mike closer & very confidently, I began to speak. "Thank you for the question. I think life, for me, is a thing to……. is a thing to….."

Crash!!!! A thing to do what?? I had no clue what to say next & I had no clue from where did those words that I had uttered come from. That's what happens when you start speaking without paying a thought. I felt as if my tongue had got tied & I was completely speechless for a couple of moments that followed. One of the judges sitting in front of me gave a 'c'mon-you-can-do-it' look, gesturing me to try again.

I did, but it proved out to be nothing more than a failing attempt. Once I lost it, I could not get it back. I began to feel embarrassed, and stole eyes from everyone. But, it could not stop them from seeing in my worst situation till then.

However, the three guys sitting in the front were angels from heaven. No less than that! To rescue me out of the ordeal, they put up another question on me. "Never mind. So, tell us about your journey in the college so far. What has it been like??"

This time, I was given around 20 seconds to formulate a good answer, or at least an answer. "I believe that our college is a wonderful place, and my journey so far has been really good. I. . . I have. ." I suddenly paused in the middle of my statement. Not again please, I prayed. But that was all I managed to speak, when just a moment ago, I had a zillions of things running in my mind, which were good enough to be spoken about.

Silence prevailed for 5 seconds, 6, 7.., 8.... Just as the moments passed, anxiety soared in me, choking me up. I tried hard to recompile my thoughts and to blurt out any sensible thing in English, but it was no cake walk for me. At least not when 200 eyes were staring at me, in the most embarrassing situation, I had been caught till then. I was putting questions to my senses, pleading them to reply & ended up cursing them. It seemed as if my brain had gone for hibernation. I felt helpless, Useless, Paralyzed. I gave up. There was no point in standing there at the stage making others enjoy my frailty any further.

"Yeah it was good, that's it." I said, returned the mike, and stepped down from stage. I was completely pale by then. I had gone numb. My chances of becoming Mr. Fresher were out of the question. I did not even bother about it. Manav was titled as Mr. Fresher that eve. I barely stood a chance after all that happened. It hardly made any difference to me.

But I hated why on earth, was English brought to my country, why?? And, if it was, then why could not I manage to mumble a few lines in it fluently. Why did it prove out to be so notorious when I least expected that to happen? I wished to forget the throat-thickening nightmare. But on the other end, I wanted to remember it forever, commit it into my memory forever. So, that it could haunt me every now & then and rake me up about how terrible I was at English.

.

When you are in college, things seem to be running. Time sprints up. Events follow another and the series becomes never-ending. Internal exams of my engineering popped up the very next week. Owing to my competitive nature, I gulped down every subject's course & performed quite well.

The internal practical's occupied us with bundles of files and papers. And, the semester exams began in no time. The 6 subjects our 1st semester offered could not be called tough by any measures. They were not, at least for species that had borne the burn of endless torturing syllabus of physics, chemistry and Maths for the past 2 years of their lives.

Our subjects were in fact very engrossing & pulled me harder to gen up more. By god's grace& my preceding guy's assistance, the exams went off well. The end of external practical's & viva-voce's concluded the 1st semester, on January 10th, 2008.

The college re-opened in the first week of February. I was fresh in my mind to start up with the 2nd semester. Almost a month at home, though I missed college a bit, but life was a thing of joy, of peace. The days passed while lying on the bed while the nights, in chatting with random people over social networking sites. I had shown my face to all my kith and kin who had declared my existence as endangered, because of my schedule during the high school.

However, I had utilized my vacations in one real good sense. I had set my mind & decided the direction of the boat I wanted to sail in. I had prepared myself for the upcoming semester & the portion of mugging that was waiting for me. 'Proper attention to knowledge'- was the 2nd semester's resolution. Learn the world beyond books, I was clear about the aim. I wanted to do well at everything, especially in academics. It is something everybody longs for, whenever a new semester commences.

Exactly from February, I had become damn sincere. I attended almost all the lectures & more importantly, listened carefully to everything being taught. I utilized the free time in the internet lab.

I could not believe Pulkit calling me nerdy, until that one day. I was taken by surprise when Tanya came up to me & asked me for the solution of a numerical. Some of her friends were entitled geeks from the Day one. So, she really did not have to. After all, geeky was their trademark.

To the weirdest of my luck, initially I got fumbled by her charisma. Tanya walking to ask me for something in a class of over 60 was surreal. I mean, even if it was for a stupid question, she really thought I could do better than others. The mere thought was enough to amuse me, and transport me to cloud nine. And all I did was flipping through pages of her notebook, and stealing sights at safe intervals. If only someone could tell her what the reason behind confusion of my mind was. It was her! But, when she said, "I thought you might know how to crack this." I tried again & succeeded.

Pulkit, sitting next to me, was apparent only after Tanya left. It would not be a lie if I state that a hundred people could go unnoticed when she stood 2 inches away from me. Pulkit winked at me, as I tried to change the topic. "Have you tried the derivations given to us?"

"Uhm, no, I thought you must be knowing how to do them." He said imitating Tanya's tone. And added sheepishly, "Mr. certified nerd."

The month of March had unexpected things in store. Things like I had never guessed. Like we had heard, the annual college fest was to be organized in the end of the march or in the first week of April. So, the preparations for it had taken a start. The techno-cultural fest meant lots of zeal, fun, & the best part, abundance of free lectures. The rest of the college was preparing skits, choreographing dance performances, singing songs, making robots, designing applications, and what not.

And my friends & I were enjoying a time of the life. Anybody rarely attended classes and so did we. Escaping out of the class had become our daily routine, by giving a believable excuse to the professors. The objective meant sitting in the cafeteria or corridors, playing and watching the commotion around us.

We were sitting in the cafeteria, forming a group when Raman, a senior called me. He was one of the guys involved in our fresher's party. He gestured me to come out of the group. I did as he asked me to do, making an excuse to my friends.

"Hey." He said, as we shook hands.

"Hi. How were you, sir??"

"I'm doing fine. Did not see you after the party?? The star's too busy, I guess." He made a dig at me.

"Don't embarrass me, sir. I was just occupied by exams."

"Yeah, I see. People do study a lot in the 1st year, a lot."

I nodded. "And after that??"

He laughed at my question as I felt that I had ridiculed him. "You'll know it by yourself, man. So, what's up?? Must be performing at the fest??"

I gave him a 'do-my-face-look-like-I-can' look. "Uhm, not really." I said and thought of the possible things I could do to entertain the mass. My technical skills were not even in their infancy. I was a singer by no chance, and taking my dancing abilities into consideration, accepting me could not be called for any group as a real grace. And acting would be such a nightmare for the viewers.

"Tell me, would you like to perform??"

"As in??"

"I mean playing keyboard. Do you know we have a 'battle of bands' competition too??"

I thought for a couple of seconds & then answered, "Yeah, I have heard, a bit though." Of course, I had not, but I was in no state to say 'no' to that. Especially, after the kind of expression that he wore, I did not want to let him down and consider me ignorant either.

"Good. Look, many bands have proved their mettle on the performance ground, & I tell you, it's a great opportunity." He said things that were too convoluted for me to grasp. "Aryan, let's make it easier. I can recommend you to a band, if you want."

"Really?? Is it possible??"

"Hmmm. Everything is. And you must, must go for it." He sounded really convincing. "And you'll learn a lot with them, if things go smooth."

"Sure if you say so. Then I would like you to talk to them. Go ahead, sir."

"Wonderful..!"

Two days later, I was informed by Raman that a music band called 'Vishesh' wanted to hear me.

"You know that these guys are mostly coming from the 2nd year itself." Raman said, as we climbed up the staircase to make our way to the practice room.

"Ohh?? So, all of them??"

"Yes, except the guitarist who is from the final year. But they are really good guys, adjustable people. If you get chosen, you'll have long way to go." He said, while I was trying to keep composed and not to worry.

"Sir, is there any requirement in their band?? I mean, for a keyboard player??"

"Not actually, but they have promised me that they can accommodate a keyboard player, if they find you to be up to the mark." He said, pointing me to the room. I nodded. I played 2 songs of my choice, just like they have asked me to. And to be honest, they were much different from what I had expected them to be. No arrogance, no superiority.

After spending half an hour with them, I could remark that there was a sense of stability had made home in those guys, something that I lacked, that most of the people I have known before lacked. However, in no sense, it could be inferred as they were dull. They made fun of each other, pulled my legs, and played music for joy, their real joy.

After my turn, they played a song together, quite enjoyable. I had not heard that song before, but they had surely made good music through it. They asked me, if I could try playing that song too. But, I told them honestly that it was the first time I had heard that one.

Like I thought, without making any complaints, they were sweet enough to play it again for me. And even help me along the performance. After a few trials, I was able to catch up the rhythm and I succeeded in playing the 1st snippet of the song. I was enjoying it.

"That sounds impressive, man." Their lead singer said, after I could play the song without much assistance. I was happy to get appreciated. Who isn't?

"It is. So, from when you have been playing the keyboard." Their drummer asked me.

"Some 5-6 years, sir. As far as I can remember from std. 8th!"

He smiled & said, "Very good. It shows you had."

"Aryan, we do consider you're really skilled, but…." One of them spoke and shook his head.

I raised my eyebrows, waiting him to complete and wondering what that shaking of head meant. Why do people take pauses & kill others with suspense when they are not ought to do that? I finally asked, "But??"

"Do you have another keyboard?? Larger than this one??"

"No, this is the only one I possess right now."

"Actually, none of us has any doubt about your potential to fit with us. In fact, we have rarely ever seen someone playing that good in his 1st year. But, what bothers us is that your keyboard is somewhat smaller than a stage performance's requirement."

"Ohhh!! So, this one won't work." I was disappointed.

"If it would, then we would have been happier. But unfortunately, it won't. Can you get a new one?? Or can you arrange it from somebody else??"

I thought for a while. "I don't know, sir. I would need to think. But, I have performed on this SA-21 many a time."

"Of course, but there's a lot of difference between an individual performance & a band performance, no. See, if you're able to get it, it'll surely help you in future too." One of the guitarists said, trying to convince me.

"You're right." I nodded. "Sir, I'll surely try. I'll make up my mind, and inform you."

"Sure."

After I left their room, I thought about what happened inside. May be I should get another one. May be I should not. Dad would hardly say 'no', if I push him even a lil. So, the decision relied upon me.

Yes, they were good musicians, but a larger keyboard would cost around Rs. 20000.May be even more than that. Was a mere stage performance in my college worth that amount, I wondered. Plus, I would have to practice along with them throughout the day, missing out all fun that my rest classmates will have. And, still it might not end up anywhere. I may not be able to match up with their work.

I was not willing to buy the keyboard. To say the least, I chuck out the thought that I was offered by a band called 'Vishesh'.

We were free & untamed as birds in those days. And, the 'study-hard-and-alike' promises I had made at the beginning of the semester got buried in their graves unannounced. But there was something which really bothered the hell out of me sometimes. Tanya had been a part of her group quite from the first month of the college, but now there was something unusual when she sat with them. Noticeable indeed!

Most of the times, she was with Manav. Always with him. And even while they sat in a group, a few sparks could be seen flying between the two of them. I often pondered what I felt when I saw them together. Some sort of creepy feeling, that flared up my interiors. I wanted to tell her something, may be to stay away. But then, who was I to do that. It was her life, I guess.

I never guessed before!!

The much awaited annual fest began on the eve of 29th march. We were all really excited as it was the 1st annual fest of our engineering life. Watching the college decorated beautifully with pools of lights all around made our spirits soar. The stage's background was completed by the largest possible & the most beautiful canvas anyone had ever witnessed in their lives, making it the heart of the college.

There was a feeling of happiness, pride, ecstasy, with pangs of expectations rising higher every second. The atmosphere was never better before. The performances began at around 11:30 a.m. Performers from many other colleges had also come, making it a grand show & to provide a neck-to-neck competition as well.

They all exhibited their remarkable talent, making the 1st day flawless. And, in the war among performers, the art & the audiences always win. We got to see ultimate breathe-taking performances.

The second Day of the fest meant events like the skits & the musical performances. 'Battle of bands' was one of them. As per I had heard, 4 bands from other colleges, and 2 from ours were going to participate. I had heard a lot about one, the final year's band. Also, a new called 'Vishesh' was joining that year. Quite unknowingly, I had a deep desire to watch a band performance. I wanted to see how these guys performed.

Occasionally, the 'battle of bands' began with G.N.C.T's band performance at 6:30 p.m... It was the 1st time I was watching any band performing live in front of my eyes. And watching meant believing! To my surprise, a band performance was much more than I thought. Every passing second made me feel curious about what to come next. After G.N.C.T and E.L. College's performance, 'VISHESH' came to light.

VISHESH's performance began with the 12-minutes-long sound check. After which they performed their 1st song. The appreciation they got from the audiences put the 1st two performances into shade. The crowd went even crazier, as they took off further. The supreme performance made the audiences roar and roar. It was really that good.

I could see them all, their faces glowing. That moment made them resemble stars. Real stars, who could make others mad for themselves, who were capable making others die to swap positions with them. I so wanted to be one of them, performing at the stage. That was when I realized that I had committed a blunder in my sheer ignorance. I must have gone berserk to say 'no' to Vishesh.

I could be one of them, and I got the chance so easily. But call it my childishness or stupidity, I slapped the opportunity in its face. Even Pulkit understood that it was. His one statement was enough to make me feel guiltier. He said, "Look at them. You would have surely lost it, man, when you denied them."

How could I be so oblivious to their potential?

While Vishesh performed, everybody could see them, so did I. but, for them I was another face in the crowd, that might not be able to get recognized. And, I was responsible for that to happen. I had 1 answer with me by then. Yes, a performance like that was worth the price of a new keyboard. It was not a 'mere' performance. I wished I could go back & stop myself from declining the golden chance, but life's not that easy, I guess. It was too late to regret, too late to ponder.

After 'Vishesh' stepped down, the final year's band 'Zenith' came to perform. And if Vishesh was magic, they were supernatural. A hundred words of praise for them looked justified. In fact, they deserved more. Their performance had the guts to set the stage on fire. They were the epitome of stardom, of celebrations, of life.

Fate had taught me a lesson that I could not fail to remember. That night, when Vishesh had the world fallen at their feet, I sat in darkness till 2 A.M. replaying Vishesh's performance in my mind over and again, and waiting for dear slumber to give me some peace. But, I hardly fell asleep till the moment I made a promise to myself.

Life after the fest rolled on to the way it was in the month of February. I wanted something to focus on. And what could be better than internal exams for that. I worked harder, and scored well.

Even apart from internal practical, I tried to stay on my toes, making myself aware. At college, rest of the things occupied us. From mid-may itself, our 'preparatory leaves' or the popularly called P.L.'s began.

However, the name I feel is a misnomer for most of the engineering students in our country. For us, calling them as 'semi-vacations' would be more appropriate. During the P.L.'s, my schedule was much familiar to the one I had in my winter break after the 1st semester exams, except for one necessary change. The long night chats were replaced by long night gen ups. After all, studying was the need of the hour.

My result for the 1st semester was out & I had scored 75.8%, which meant I was ranked no.4 in my class. It was something that I did not like. Perhaps, it pushed me to gulp more and more chapters. With all my preparations, I waited for the last exams of 1st year. As per the convention, after the final practical, the 2nd semester got winded up by the end of June.

Another beautiful time of our lives awaited for us as the almost 2-month long stretched vacations got winded up. The 2nd year of our college life, of our engineering, had taken a start. I was really very keen to look forward to it. For no longer, we could be called as 'freshers'. We were finally the seniors.

There's 1 thing about growing up in college life. A distinct feeling of pride comes along with getting older. Or at least, we felt something cool about it. No more chances of 'giving intros in cafeterias', no more 'alienated' looks, no more references 'just-out-school-kids'.

Nevertheless, now we are the one making fun of the 1st year's guys in every possible manner. This is a universal fact. Everybody, no matter how nerdy or how spoilt they are at their time, love doing deep analysis on the childishness spread over their juniors, for at least once.

The 3rd semester brought to me 4th October, 2008, my most awaited birthday. I was keen like never before since it gave me an undying opportunity to ask for a keyboard as my birthday present from mom and dad. I had reasoned that the keyboard I possessed from 3 years had become too small for me. But, the moment when I told them about the offer I got, it did wonders for me. A Yamaha-410 keyboard became mine on the very next day.

The excitement for my newly-owned prized possession magnetized me to home. I bunked the last lectures almost for a week & returned home early to play the keyboard, which burned a hole of Rs. 17,650 in dad's pocket.

Not just the excitement, the gusto escalated, as the years progressed, the group-ism in our class rose touched the sky. And so did the flame wars. It was lunch time. We were all beginning to eat our meals in the classroom, when 4 of our classmates went to the dais. Manav, Ankit, Tanya, Rohit.

Before anyone of us could figure out what their motive was, Manav began to announce, "guys, we have a news for you all. All of us knew that we had to organize a fresher's party in the 2nd year. So, we have decided to make it possible on 22nd October, 11:00 a.m. The venue is hotel Madrid." He said all that in almost one breath.

Though his becoming Mr. Fresher made very lil difference to me, but every glance of that guy after he became Tanya's 'closest friend' tortured me. The 'Tanya' thing was really thorny.

"Guys, the juniors have given a really nice feedback & are thoroughly thrilled. Those want to come and join us…… "

"When did they manage to plan all this??" Pulkit asked to me, as they continued to rant about 'the' plan.

"I'm equally clueless." I said to him.

"And what is she doing behind him??" Pulkit said, looking at Tanya, as if she asked for my exclusive permission to walk up there. I made a face and just shrugged.

"Please deposit the money before this 14th if you are interested, so that we can make the down payments on time." Manav's utter confident tone when he said those words was so sky-rocketed as if the director of the college himself had given them the authority to host the party. Then, he added as an afterthought, "Any queries??"

Nobody answered back. It seemed as if they had turned into statues. "Guys, you can ask if you have any kind of queries, please." The same silence yet again. But it was going wrong. Were they deaf?? I could not afford to let him go & becoming a hero, was what I knew. At least, not this time.

He said, "Alright then. So, I'd take it as its all clear. Tha..n…k… "

"I have a query." I said, stopping him in the middle of him statement, as I got up from my seat.

"Go ahead." He said with a nod.

"Tell me, do we all appear as fools out here??" I said, in a no-nonsense tone, taking wind out of Mr. Manav. His disciples who stood behind him at the dais were equally stunned, Tanya the most observable among them.

"What?? What do you mean by that??" he said.

"Oh. In case, I'm not very clear, let me elaborate, dear. Do we look like fools who are just here to get invited for the same fresher's part for which every one of us is equally responsible, but you took the charge."

"Excuse me, Aryan. Someone had to. But why do you think you people are not involved."

"Because we are not. And it's because a few snobs think that we are not capable of managing it."

"Oh really?? So that's what you think. Huh??"

"Whatever. But, I assume that there's hardly one who has perceived the idea that way. They don't have any problem. Do they??" He said, looking towards the rest of the classmates.

Oh god, this jerk should try in politics. Engineering is such a waste of his time, I wondered.

"Ok. So, let's find out that. Guys, all those who are keen & supportive about the fresher's eve arranged by our very dear friends, please, raise your hands." I announced, sarcasm in my voice reflected. Three of my classmates raised their hands.

"And now those who are not in favor of the party just announced and would want things to take a turn, please raise your hands." I had almost made an estimate of what was going to come out, before I spoke that statement. I had crossed my fingers.

Around 13 or 14 people came up. The rest of our classmates looked like they hardly had any interest in the world around them. The number was quite less than the expected, but thank god, we still led in the ratio.

"It is visible. You can see the truth." I smirked towards Manav. His complexion turned almost red. What a snapshot moment it was!

And then, Tanya finally took the charge," Look guys, it's evident that you people are hurt, but we had no such intentions. Aryan, you have really interpreted as wrong." A chill ran down my spine as she mentioned my name. I tried to keep my expression as calm as I could. In less than a moment, the anger, furiousness went missing.

Say something, goddamit, my senses told me. But what could I say to her?? Even though she was supporting an arrogant swine, scolding a girl who possessed such cute eyes was not my cup of tea. And the cuteness manifolds, every time they got widened. I tried to suppress my blushing smile, and find some words to save myself from Pulkit's upcoming scoffs.

Before I could manage to say anything, one of my classmates spoke, "No Tanya, Aryan's right. We have an equal say. It's matter of our entire class." "And we can't be denied from that." They were all finally speaking for themselves.

"But….." She tried to defend, but hardly found anything to say in defense. Even Manav fell short of words. His heroism, his over-confidence had evaporated.

"But, yes, if someone tries to deny us, we can make sure that the juniors take off their hands from any bullshit. They would prefer turning down 4 seniors rather than going against the rest majority." I said.

He said, "Guys, try & understand. We have committed & planned everything. You can't ruin them."

"We couldn't only if you had bothered asking us before doing that. But sad to say, but your plans had a short life."

"But you guys are welcomed to get involved, even in the organizing team." He said. What was that now, compensation or compromise. Nobody reacted to that. Our silence was a tight slap at their face, at their egos. It must have been harder for Manav the mastermind. Ahh!

After a couple of minutes, Manav finally uttered, "That's it. Do what you want, guys. You can organize the party all by yourself. None of us will intervene." Not only us, but his friends too were shocked from what he was saying.

"Are you sure??" I said, thoroughly enjoying the spicy moment.

"Damn sure! Note my words. We'll meet you at the fresher's." He said. His friends would have wanted to murder him for promising that. But it was too late.

"In that case, thank you so much."

We were all contented. We were merry because we had restored our right to organize the fresher's party. But I was happy because I had given it back to that weird smug. I had finally brought him down, when he was on a trip of his own.

At our turn to organize the fresher's party, we tried and involved everyone who was interested. We discussed and then decided, whether it was the date, timings, theme, or the events. Anyone could not be given any chance to point out fingers on us, I had made sure. In duration of just 3 days, we were able to put everything in to order & make the occasion a real success. Even though Manav arrived on the party eve, but his grave expressions throughout spoke out how forced his presence was. Watching the entire charge in our hands, he got irritated even more. And there she was, Ms. Tanya supporting her best friend. She did not leave his side, not even for once. If only I could know, why did she have to do everything I hate!

The end of October brings a pleasant breeze in the air, when the winter is in its advent. And laziness too! Pulkit & I were climbing up the staircase to reach our classroom in the 2rd lecture.

"Do you know about the 'talent hunt'??" he said. Our class room was at the 3rd floor and still 2 floors away.

"Yeah, I do. I won the 'people with craziest best friend' round there??" I mocked.

"Oho. Well-deserved. Congratulations, you jerk."

"Thank you, dear. But which talent hunt??"

"That's what I call sheer ignorance." He said.

"Yeah, do you realize I had not attended college from past two days??" I said justifying myself like and offended kid.

"And even then you have full detailed information about your girl. From 'what she ate in those 2 days' to 'with whom she ate'." He said. I wished if I'm granted one murder, I would not have need much time to decide. It has to be his.

"Whatever. I'm not a stalker. Why would I care what she's up to? I'm least interested now."

"Really? Nice attempt to fool the guy who stays with you throughout the day. Then, why do you steal eyes from her?"

"I don't, and if I do, it's probably because I don't want her to have any misconceptions." I said matter-of-factly.

"Whatever."

"OK, let's come out of it. Actually, it's College's Talent Hunt. They are organizing it from this year. Music, dance, oratory and stuff like that."

"Really?? And why aren't we participating in something?? "

"Because it's only for 1st year people. Not for the seniors."

"Oh I see. But it'll be good fun. It should have clicked them a year ago."

"Yeah, I wished that too. But we can watch it at least." He said, as I pondered over something else, much more important.

"You want to say something??" he asked me, as I nodded. He raised his eyebrows to enquire what was on my mind, as I said, "Uhm. We will for sure."

The talent hunt was held on 7th November, and I really felt something good came out of it apart from just 'fun.' There were many engrossing events but one thing that pulled me the most was that a band's performance. 'VISHESH's! Even when one of their mates had left the college, the four managed to make it a success. Their performance had been a feast to ears, but what thrilled me the most was a ray of hope for me. I could still give it a try. I could be easily accommodated in the band considering their requirements.

Kunal was not just VISHESH's lead vocalist but had also become an acquaintance through Raman. He was aware of my musical capabilities. I approached him and informed him that I had managed to get myself new keyboard. It was the way for me to go ahead with them, when he said, “Why don’t you join us the coming weekend? We guys practice here.”

I reached college exactly at 11 a.m. following Kunal’s instructions. Since it was a weekend, the campus looked deserted except for the hostel-residing species who were wandering around motivelessly. Besides, only the love-birds could be spotted sitting hand-in-hand all over the place. Interestingly, the love birds even outnumbered the hostlers. I felt unusually nice about being there. A corner of my heart fancied of me sitting with Tanya. But my spoilsport mind brought me back to ruthless reality, and I prayed that I don’t find her sitting with that Manav.

On reaching the practice room, I greeted everyone. Even though I was a bit more comfortable with them than I was the 1st time, I was shivering a bit. Tushar amongst them came up & shook hands with me, as he said, “Remember Tushar, no??”

“Of course, Sir. I’m Aryan.” I said, as he nodded. Tushar introduced Sandy and Vishal, rest of his band mates to me. Just as the conversation proceeded, my nervousness fled away, comforting me.

“Hmmm. So, Kunal told that you have even got a new keyboard.” Tushar asked me as we all settled down.

“That’s true. I have got it a month back.” I said, as I opened up my bag when they asked me to.

I was delighted when they said approvingly, “This can really work wonders for us.”

I played a song on my new keyboard, when Kunal asked me, contenting them about my ease with the new keyboard.

Although I knew well that one of their mates was done with engineering, I asked Tushar, “Sir, if I’m not wrong, there were five people in your band last year, right?” There was definitely some sort of space in ‘Vishesh’, Raman had already told me time and again.

“Yes Aryan, one of our band-mates left and ‘Vishesh’ needs a new bass guitarist.” Tushar said.

"Lead guitarist, yes. Rhythm guitarist, yes. But I had never heard of a ‘Bass guitarist’ till then, but how do I reveal that to them. The last I wanted was to make an impression of a naive frog in a small well. My wicked mind suggested me to beat the bush. But, a bad impression would not be as harmful as a false one, at least here. I shunned off all the nasty ideas and gathered courage to inform Tushar, "I'm afraid to say that I don't really know what makes a bass guitar differ from the normal guitar. Honestly, today is the 1st time I have heard of it."

"Never mind." He smiled and then played something with the upper strings of the guitar he was holding.

"I think I can play this through my keyboard." I said, after listening carefully.

"Keyboard?? Are you sure??" Tushar asked me.

"I suppose, Just give me some time." I said, promisingly.

After searching through the guide provided with the keyboard, I found the bass category with couple of bass options like sine bass, guitar bass, etc. I played them one by one. Finally, out of the options, the sine bass matched it up the most. After couple of minutes, I played the similar sound.

As I finished playing, all three of them looked pleased, Kunal, more than anyone else. It was written on his face.

"Sounds really good. What do you have to say??" Tushar said, as I ended.

"Truly convincing. We can consider it." Sandy said.

They discussed with each other & finally showed me a green signal & a world of happiness. I was welcomed with open arms by them.

Once while practicing on a weekend, Tushar asked me "Aryan, may I ask what made you drop the idea of performing last year?? I mean you can answer if you don't mind. Nothing hard & fast."

"No, it's OK. I think I was too ignorant. And my ignorance made me commit a huge mistake unknowingly. I lost that opportunity, but when I saw you people again on the talent hunt, all my regrets seemed to get vanished." I said.

I could see all of them smiling. "You have a great potential, dude. There is hardly any suspicion about that." Sandy said.

"True, buddy. We have to walk together for long, I hope. " Tushar said, as he smiled.

"So do I, Sir." I said.

In a nick of time, I became comfortable with them. I became a part of 'Vishesh'. Not just that we played music together, we ate together, laughed together. Music had created an invisible bond between us, piling us together.

When you are in semester system, time flies with the wings. Our result for the 2nd semester turned out, and I had succeeded in getting an aggregate of 77%. Meanwhile our semester exams soon approached. And we shifted the weight of our preference to studies for some days. The rest of my band-mates were equally competitive and conscious about their studies.

I did not want music to become a distraction in my academics. None of us did. So, we halted the practice & pulled up our socks, this time to study. I studied hard & did well on my part. The 3rd semester got over. But my craving for real music had taken its start.

The morning of 26th February brought us back to our second home, J.M.I.T. The college welcomed us for the 4th semester. Being accepted as a part of Vishesh, my spirits were high. This semester is going to be more than usual, I had borne in mind from day one. The even semesters did offer a jackpot, the annual fest.

It took around 10 days for all five of us to get united & hit the practice ground, as the rest of my mates were a year senior to me. Their devotion towards practices was responsible for the breath-taking performances, I guess. Within days, the preparations for the fest begin in the college.

Unlike last time, I was pretty much conscious of what I wanted to do. Music was what I saw myself with. Vishesh was clear about how to make their performance a bench-mark. And die-hard practice was the key.

The fest was 23 days away as we had begun practicing the songs finalized by Tushar. Had never been a part of a music band, things were quite new for me. But lucky as I was, all of my mates behaved patiently. Going by our preparations, we could bet our hard work's going to pay.

The fest must have been around 14 days away. Kunal started rehearsing the final song of the performance, while the rest 4 of us were playing our instruments.

"No, Kunal, the scale of the song should be higher. You're not getting any close to it." Tushar said to Kunal, just as he completed the first part. Kunal nodded & sang again, this time on a higher scale.

"Just not like that. I suppose you have not been able to hear it thoroughly??"

"Dude, I have heard & practiced it continuously for the past 2 hours. But I'll try again. " Kunal said & tried another time. For once, twice, thrice, but no matter how many times he tried, he could not please Tushar.

Undoubtedly, Tushar had grand sense of music, but with my knowledge, I really felt that Kunal was doing justice to the song. With every trial, Tushar's patience seemed to get extinguished, making him hyper. Kunal was still trying to refine himself until the moment Tushar blasted out on him.

"What the heck is so wrong with you, goddammit? Can't you just concentrate on what the song desires??" he shouted at the top of his voice. I was pretty shocked by the bizarre behavior, but Kunal looked shaken. Silently, he kept staring into Tushar's now-grown-red eyes. Breaking the silence after a short while, he said, "No, I can't"

"What do you mean by 'I can't'?? You have to understand how important this is. Do you get it? I just can't let go of my band's performance because of a ......" Tushar stopped amid of his statement.

"Just because of a what?? Complete what you were about to say. Speak up." Kunal rebutted. It was Tushar's turn to keep mum now.

"Kunal, Tushar, forget it, guys. It's just that we need a break." Sandy and Vishal got up from their places, and stood up between the two of them, Vishal signaling me to keep Kunal away.

"Kunal Sir, calm down. It is OK, we can sort it out peacefully." I said, trying to pacify Kunal, as Vishal and Sandy tried to bring Tushar back to his senses.

“No, Aryan. Let him finish. Tushar, let me make it clear that I too possess some intellect for music. ”

“Yes, you do and that’s why you end up singing like crap.” Tushar said.

“What?? I’m the vocalist of this band & now you come & tell me that my voice is a crap.” It was all going wrong, mistaken. “I’m no way tolerating this bullshit.” Kunal added, now turning away from Tushar & looking towards me. He was really hurt.

“Why are you telling this to him?? Say it on my face if you have guts.” Tushar said.

“Tushar, what are you….” Sandy tried to intervene.

“Let me complete, Sandy. I just don’t understand what you think you are. Oh man, peep out of this bloody room, we’ll find another hundred singers like you. We’ll get one for ‘Vishesh’ too. So, for god’s sake, get lost. ”

Kunal was baffled by all that he heard. Not just that Tushar was his band-mate, but a dear friend too. I have noticed that even when I was not even a part of ‘Vishesh’. But, with that, Tushar had crossed all his limits, broken all the bonds. It was then I realized that this was not a usual quarrel. It was going to have a massive impact.

Kunal gathered the courage to speak & said, “I can’t believe you could say that.” He looked towards the door.

“Kunal, don’t be stupid. Wait a second.” Vishal said.

“Yeah, Tushar Sir is just annoyed a lil. He did not mean anything.” Even when I told that to Kunal, in my own heart, I felt that I was lying.

“Ahm, I think I should leave now.” Kunal’s tone was turned from furious to forlorn.

“Thank you, so much. And take my words. We can perform without you, you’ll see very soon.”

“It makes no difference to me from now.” Kunal said, smashing the door, as he left the practice room. Neither Sandy nor Vishal could stop him from leaving. But it was going to make a difference to Kunal, I knew. A huge difference!

After Kunal left, 'Vishesh' was shattered to smithereens. Without the vocalist, a band becomes voiceless and soulless too. Tushar must have realized that, but he did not admit it in front of us. Vishal & I tried hard to convince but Kunal did not change his mind. Our attempts were not enough to bring Kunal back. But we had to perform at any cost. We could not step back. Our probe for a new vocalist took over us.

One day, I suggested, "There's a guy in my class who sings pretty well."

Tushar raised his eyebrows and said as an afterthought, "What's his name??"

"Ameesh. But I wonder if he'll be willing to perform, but chances are that he will."

"Hmmm, just give him a call." Tushar said anticipation in his eyes. I nodded.

Our search for a new vocalist got extinguished in the form of Ameesh. I was happy when I introduced him to Vishesh, but I was happier that we would be able to perform now.

With Ameesh's entry, the destiny made someone else arrive too, Rohit. Ameesh & Rohit were best friends & Rohit knew how to play guitar. Ameesh convinced Tushar by telling him that Rohit would willingly buy a bass guitar. His achievement of getting a bass guitarist for Vishesh made Tushar's happiness burst at the seams.

The 6 of us started practicing wholeheartedly. My job was to provide bass, but given that 'Vishesh' had found a bass guitarist, things began to get rough for me. I had never imagined that Rohit's coming could put my presence in shade. But it did. Needless to say, my existence in 'Vishesh' was inversely proportion to his growing importance.

Rohit had an upper hand over me, so more or less I was snubbed as 'no longer required'. It was not something I felt, but something they all made me realize. Whatever I did, they criticized it. Even my friendship with Kunal had begun to bother thick-headed Tushar, overnight.

What Vishesh wanted from me had become a riddle wrapped up in enigma, which was no way easy to figure out.

Even after Tushar said to me, "we're practicing, you can sit over & see where ever you can manage to give some score." I tried every bit of mine to retain my position. 'To give some score' was the only consolation I was given. But, for me, everybody's behavior prevaricated. They stopped reacting, let alone suggesting something to me. I had never seen such a sea change. The worst fell when it started feeling like I was not even present in that practice room. Nobody even bothered to talk to me.

I tried to win their confidence by trying to provide lead background from the keyboard, but I was taken aback when they said, "it sounds like cacophony." Even though, I knew well it was of no use, I did not give up. But, every attempt I made went in vain. Absolutely futile. I had become a toy to mock at. While I sat there every day alone watching them practice, overlooking my presence, Ameesh & Rohit were over the moon. Whatsoever I played or suggested, they hardly missed any opportunity to ridicule it.

But, my heart got pierced when I over-heard Tushar saying to Rohit, "When will we get rid of this prick? Can't he just realize that he's hardly needed anymore?" Those words took life out of me. People I called 'friends' stabbed my back and gave me nothing except betrayal.

That day, I got to know what I meant for 'Vishesh'. I meant an irritation, a pain in the neck. I realized I could be anything but not a stalker. The same band which had welcomed me with open arms, made me feel like an extra, recluse stalker. An outsider! I did not watch their performance, I ran

That day, either my patience gave up or my conscience got woken. I told them that I won't be a waste-of-time distraction in their practice sessions any longer. I plucked out the wires out of my keyboard, threw them in front of them & walked off. Good riddance, I heard Rohit say aloud, just as I stepped out.

The invisible bond that stood between 'VISHESH' and me had got converted in to an invisible barrier which could not be crossed, no matter what I tried. Everything I scared turned in to reality. I could feel Kunal's hurt. That night, my relationship with 'Vishesh' came to an end. End in its most tragic forms.

For life goes on!!

I did not want to return back to college, but Pulkit forced me to come. I kept trying to hide, to run, but he would never allow me to. He made me understand that I could not escape for longer & staying idle at home will only worsen things. At college, everyone was engrossed in things they loved. I was thrown out of mine.

Music was my craving. It helped me think and everything else seemed like mere options. I tried to get involved in an event or the other, but nothing heals when your heart is somewhere else. But, I had to pose happy & unaffected, making my classmates or anyone who knew me believe that I could do well without 'Vishesh'. I wanted to watch them perform and applause at them, so that people don't deem me as a limping loser.

On the second day of the fest, when 'Vishesh' was about to perform, the destiny had another drill prepared for me to pass, Pulkit & I were assigned the duty of managing the backstage itself. While Tushar, Vishal, Sandy, Ameesh& Rohit were excited for their performance, I wanted to run away from there to a distant place, from where I could not take a single glance of them.

But at exteriors, I tried to maintain composure. I could see an igniting spark in their eyes, while mine were paining. When I saw Ameesh noticing me, I signaled a thumbs-up & passed a wide smile to him. They went ahead to perform. I took everything in my stride & then tried to get occupied in some activity, so that I did not get time to feel sick.

March 31st, 2010.

The final day of the fest brought me face to face with many things. At 8:00 pm. It had become really dark, but the luminosity of the lights made every corner of the college gleam.

"Buddy, let's go that side."Rajat said, as we watched the show.

"Hmmm. Something wrong here??" I asked him back, still looking at the engrossing play being performed.

"Not actually. But from there, the view will be a better." Rajat said. I was in no mood to protest, so we proceeded to the location he wanted. Just as we reached there, a girl popped up from a group and advanced towards Rajat.

After they had shook hands, passed smiles, and exchanged eye-to-eye ciphers, Rajat introduced her as Parul. From a couple of months, I too had heard that Rajat & a junior girl called Parul were smitten. But it was the first time, I was meeting her. So, by now I knew why my friend was so desperate to come to that side.

"Ohh. So Rajat sir, what take you so long to travel across 20metres??"Parul asked him, exercising her 'typically girl-friend' rights on him.

"Actually, we liked it more there, so… " Rajat said, teasing her back.

"Ohoho! Poor you, I guess."

I stared at the stage, waiting for the play Pulkit was going to act in, without disturbing the 'lover birds', while they enjoyed pulling each other's legs. Unfortunately, it was 2-3 performances away, Pulkit informed me by the text. Quite soon, they realized that he had a friend present there too. They involved me by cracking a few jokes about the performance carried out.

"Sir, that girl in blue is my room-mate & best friend." Parul told me pointing towards the announcer, just as a performance got winded up.

I wondered about how to react to that. So, I smiled back and said a mild "okie" to her. Before I could make any analysis over her, she stepped down, completing her job. Ms. Blue appeared on the stage a couple of another time, after that. Far as she was, it was not quite possible to make out how she exactly looked, but I could say that she was not utterly fair, but neither that dark in complexion. As it appeared to me, she resembled Parul, but only shorter than her. Her command over the language I dreaded from the years was definitely 0impressive.

“Sir, my friend wants to come here, but she is a bit hesitating to come here.” Parul said to me, as the performances went over. I nodded & thought for a while. Hesitating? Do I bite, I wondered. May be a stranger was the reason for her discomfort.

“Oh! That’s OK, I won’t mind leaving if you want. ” I said, still wondering about the awkward situation that made me perceive myself as a ‘woman-eater’.

“No. you got me wrong.” She said, protesting.

“Then, guys??” I asked her back, as she made another secretive gesture to her boyfriend.

Following her expressions, Rajat said, “Dear, you can go & check if your friend is searching for you. Let me explain.”

“So, tell me lover-boy, what did your beloved just try to say??” I winked at him, just as he turned to me.

He blushed for a second & said, “Well, she meant that someone’s being in great demand.”

“Who?? Demand as in??”

“For some girl. The same one who’s feeling nervous to come in front of you.”

“Hold on, man, what does that imply??” I asked him as I felt something fishy going on.

Before he could answer me back, Parul arrived with this ‘I’m very scared of you’ chic. It was that same announcer Parul told me about a few minutes ago. After she greeted Rajat, and then she looked at me, but fell silent. Finally after 5 seconds, I said a ‘hiii’ to her to ease out the silence.

“Sirat, he’s my friend, Aryan.” Rajat said, as she smiled, looking straight in to my eyes. The dark eye make-up she had worn looked relevant and was fairly noticeable.

“I really loved you at the stage. Awesome.” Parul said pampering her best friend. Only girls, I suppose, are the species who are capable of promoting public display of affection so easily.

“Yuppi. Thank you.” She answered, as Parul looked at me with expecting eyes.

“Uhm. She’s right. Nice job, Sirat” I complemented her as well.

“Sirat.” She smiled and then added in her extra-sweet tone, “Thanks a lot, sir. Now I can believe that it went well.”

“’Now you can believe’, huh?? So, Ms. Sirat does not believe my words.” Parul said, pulling her legs.

“May be I can.” She chuckled, as Rajat grinned. Witty best friend and giggling boyfriend are not too a pleasing combination. Poor Parul.

Then Sirat added, “No idiot, it’s that you praise me everything I do, but now I have got one confirmation, no.”

Looking at the way she teased Parul, it was quite unbelievable to imagine the same girl feel shy to come in front of me, just a couple of minutes ago.

Finally, it was my best friend & his group’s turn to perform. I had seen the rehearsals a couple of times, but their act was magical enough to keep anyone’s eyes stayed glued to the stage for the next few minutes.

“Aryan” Sirat said as the performance ended, as I threw her a look, “Aryan sir, you played an instrument in the fresher’s party, didn’t you??”

“I did, but how do you know, you too are from??”

“Computers department.” She said, as we both smiled.

“Oh good.”

So, after a few minutes, she asked “So, did you perform in the fest??”

“No, not this time.” I said, wishing she would not dig in to the matter anymore in my heart of hearts.

“But why n…” She said as I made an excuse, without letting her complete that I had an urgent call to make. I walked aside, and called up Pulkit to ask him, if he could make it faster. But, the noise around him made it difficult to understand what he spoke.

I told Rajat that Pulkit was waiting for me somewhere, so I headed away from them, biding an adieu.

I left because I dreaded that Sirat might ask me something that I would not want to answer. After all, I was not answerable to the girl who had flown in just a couple of minutes ago. And the last thing I wanted to happen was ruining my own mood to give some strange chic a topic for gossip, and Pulkit to reach them.

Life after the fest rolled on to the usual mugging up schedule, internals, and results. Our date-sheet for the 4th semester exams came out the following week. Yes, it was like the toughest semester that we have been offered so far. But, I had done enough in the 4th semester to ensure that my preparations were next to nil. But my only consolation was that exams were almost a month away. So, from the next morning itself, I made sure that books ruled life for a month at least.

I scheduled myself in the ocean of engineering books. When the exams begin, it seems like the universal time unit has got condensed secretly. Days seemed shorter than ever. And it looked like the 4th one was the shortest semester of my engineering life. Exams wrapped up in a blink of eye, but that was what I desired honestly.

I was keen about my internship that began within the very next week. Like most of my classmates, I had got myself a seat in an institution in Chandigarh. Who wants to lose a chance to stay in the nearest beautiful city (nonetheless 100 km away from home) for 2 months? Nobody does, at least when they are 20 or given that they are completely joyless.

It was four days after my programming internship begun; I saw a few guys with a guitar and found out that a music academy was located nearby my internship institute. A passion had seeded itself inside me from a few months back, the passion to play guitar. But, since finding music tutor in a small town like ours was a hard row to hoe, my passion was crushed in no while.

But it definitely had reasons to bother me. A corner of my mind always held my inability to play this instrument responsible for getting me kicked out of Vishesh. It must have been at least one of the reasons. But things were different here, and there was no way going to lose this opportunity. So, I joined the academy the very next day.

From day one, I practiced hard and luckily, things with them turned out to be fruitful.

After I discovered that it was easy for me to touch base with guitar, I brought an acoustic guitar. My experience that followed with them totally changed my opinion & made me realize that learning a guitar was the feast I would trade my life for.

Though in the beginning, I entitled Chandigarh as a jackpot, as I could learn programming and playing guitar well, side-by-side. However, very sooner, internship inclined to become a second fiddle, and guitar a real charm.

Apart from my Guitaring, Chandigarh had succeeded in bringing a sea change in me. It, being my 1st experience of staying away from home, taught me to manage things on my own. And yes, now I could finally distinguish the blunders of my wardrobe from the wearable ones. A sneak at the older clothes was enough to horrify me of the way I dressed during the past two years. Fortunately, I had started giving a thought before I say anything & not ended up saying everything that I thought. One of the big lessons of life indeed!

But what it changed the most was my perception of things. My interaction with guitar tutor there had rooted in me a strange confidence about music. I remember his words so well when he said, "everything worth getting is never placed on the 'discount' shelves.

College started on 2nd September for the third year. And life rolled back to normalcy. No more night-outs, no more fun rides, no more day-long Guitaring, only boring classes were what we were left with. Classes, labs, and then of course the new stretched out speeches by every professor to wake us up.

In the first week, none of the professors left without giving us a 10 minute sermon. All of them advised the same thing that we had to open our eyes & start preparing for the placements, GATE, CAT, or wherever we wanted to land in the near future. On our end, it meant nothing more than nice way to kill time. Words like 'constructive', 'expertise' are no big deal when you enter in 3rd year. Are they? Like always, our class kept up with the 'bunking theory' to balance out the equations with back-breaking lectures.

Once after attending the sixth lecture, I was returning home, when I met Sirat. She was outside the library. For me, I had never been to that place after I cleared my 1st year. Her white colored suit was fairly visible from a distance. It suited her well. According to me, white is the color that suits everyone.

"What's the crowd here??" I said as she advanced towards me.

"Actually, they have put up the list of new additional books for each year. So..?" she said as I nodded.

"Oh, the lecturer's don't tell you all this in the class."

"They do. But who lends an ear to them??" She chuckled.

I gave her a look. She added "I mean, ultimately we'll have to end up coming in the library only to get them issued, no."

"Yeah, I guess. And do tell me, if I can help."

"Sir, actually, you can."

"OK. Tell me."

"Sir, do you have the book on Database Systems by Navathe?" She said, and waited me to answer. After a couple of seconds, she added, "I promise I'll return it just after this semester."

"No that, my mind was somewhere else. I'll look for it at home & tell you." I wondered how I would tell her.

"Sure, and if it helps, ask Rajat sir to inform me about it through Parul. Only if you don't mind." she said.

"Oh. I would."

"What?? Would you mind or would you tell??" she asked with a confused expression.

"The latter, of course." I said. Her lips converted into a smile.

The next day, I said to Rajat, "Hey, convey something to Sirat."

"Whattttttttt do you want to convey, man?????" He asked me as if I was disclosing the hugest of secrets.

"This! Just a book, buddy." I said as I gave him the book and made it clear that she had asked for it. Poor gossiper lost his chance, I smirked.

"Ohh. I thought that you too." He said & winked.

"Wait a second. Don't you dare tell me what you thought?" I warned him. "And give it to Parul, she'll pass it on."

"Oh. Why you mind if I give it to Sirat directly??" He said teasingly.

"Well, not me. But someone else might." I shrugged.

"Who??"

"Parul." I said and laughed, as Rajat made a disappointed face.

Music was growing in me, day by day. By now, I knew one thing. If you want to be a part of something, find ways, or better create your own. Who knows there might be others who are waiting for a door to get opened, the one you build. If you want to dance, find platform you can dance on. If you want to play sports, search for your mates, push them and go hit the courts. If you want to perform music, find your ways, your band may be & go for it. And just step ahead, because if you won't, you'll always stay in the same place. Don't wait for someone else to do something you can't live without. Music was that thing for me, so I had to find the ways leading me to it. And if not find, then create them.

Not for a day, or two, but I had given a deep thought to the venture of creating a music band on my own, but considerable number of days. Risks, opportunities, necessities, Pro's, con's, everything. And, in the most crucial decisions you have to ever make, your brain surrenders to your heart very often.

The most important thing about forming a music band meant converging all the members to a certain point, which connects them. But for making that happen, the members should exist too. So, Target 1 was searching for people who could slog to stay together. And I was ready to plump any depths for it.

College's talent hunt helped me finding a guitarist. After Jatin won the instrumentals round, he precipitated in to my preference list. He accepted my offer without any second thought. There was a guy in my sight, who had ranted in a friend's party about his drumming abilities. But I was not pretty sure about him, because, in parties like that, people often booze and do one of the two things: either exposing out everything they had ever done or flaunting & claiming about everything they had never tried before.

I really wished he did not belong to the 2nd category. Somehow, I found that guy. Though, the exercise included asking the uncountable people, who could be related to him, in any possible manner. Some threw suspected looks at me. How do you react when a guy who never asked about a girl, probing excitedly about another guy?

Finally, all is well that ends well. I met him. Arpit. "Yes, I can play drums. But this band thing is too hi-fie for me."

"Hi-fie!! Oh come on. Be confident." I said.

"Hmm. But I don't possess a drum kit. So, seems quite tough."

"Look buddy. If I get confident about your drumming abilities, I'll get the drum kit arranged." I told him.

"Aryan, are you serious??"

"Do I look like I'm not?? Of course, I'm, but I need to get assured."

"OK."

I was ecstatic when Arpit told that he had a friend who could let him play their drums. "Who is this friend? I mean anyone would rarely take the risk of putting his drum-kit in the college." I asked Arpit as a matter-of-factly.

"That's right, but he's in this band called 'Vishesh', Sandy."

"Sandy?"

"Yeah, and Sandeep actually, but he is just paranoid about being called by this name." Arpit continued talking, but I was under a shock after his previous statements. I mean, why was I destined to have close shaves with the set of people I wished to depart from this planet? Even though it was the need of the hour, I was reluctant to go back to those irritating faces and ask for anything. Even the minutest of favours from them was unforgivable. "I was wondering if I had heard about him." I said as an excuse, after Arpit shudder me from my dilemma.

“Are you really sure they’ll allow us?” I asked him, trying to keep my expression as normal as I could.

“I suppose, and it’s such a small thing that they won’t take their hands off.” he said, as I kept mum trying to figure out. I asked him, “Can’t we find some other way out?”

Arpit tried to convince me by saying, “We won’t get a drum-kit anywhere else in the college buddy. It won’t take much time. And if we go ahead, it might make things easier for us, I guess.” He made sense. I could not stand the stupidity of buying a drum-kit on the basis on assumptions. I had to think practically.

“Hmmm, so your friend won’t say no to you?” I asked him finally.

“In no case.”

Arpit made a call to Sandy and like Arpit had said, it did not take much time to ask for what we wanted. Arpit directed us to the room, where we met Sandy and Tushar. In the first moment after we entered inside, I was happy that at least the other two were not present. Rohit, undoubtedly, topped my order of preference when it came to disgust. While Arpit talked to them for a minute or two, I made sure I look totally occupied with my phone. Anything that could help me overlook their presence would do!

And then finally, Arpit played the drums for some 3-4 minutes. To be honest, he was not too good, but he was not too bad either. And chances of finding someone else for drumming were rare. After we left the room, Arpit asked what was going in my mind.

I just said one sentence. “I’ll get the drums.”

At home, I could not reveal my new wish. A new drum kit required no less than 10000 bugs. So, it was out of question. Paying this amount when their son did not even know a, b, c of it!!!! My parents were not that credulous. But luckily, the way came out of the will. I heard of an orchestra group who intended to sell their drum kit. I checked that their drums were in good condition. On some bargaining, they agreed to trade it for Rs. 5400. I brought them home with dad’s permission, and of course his money. The very next eve, I called up Arpit. He disconnected the call & texted back:

"I'm at home for some urgent work. Can't pick ur call. Will call u, just as I return after 6 days."

So, I had to prolong my wait. For another 6 days. That was what I thought, by then. Just six days!

Meanwhile, my meetings with Sirat became more frequent. Although, they could not be exactly called meetings, but stopping for a minute or two, while we passed nearby each other. She had floated from my list of 'Ignorable s' to the normal category.

All human beings have a tendency to plan everything in advance. Arpit would return in a week, Jatin is right here. We'll find a vocalist soon. I had laid a full-fledged plan in my mind. But god has his own ways to practice his powers. To ruin our plans! May be that's why he's the god, and we are mere creatures.

Two days later, my result for 4th semester came out. I had scored a.........supplementary in the subject 'Microprocessors and Interfacing.'

Shock, distress, petrified - these words were just not enough to define what I felt when I saw that devastating web page. In those initial minutes of terror, things made no sense. How could I get a supplement?? The exam went OK, if not great, but a supplement was the least I expected. The least I deserved.

Hundreds of thoughts took birth in my mind, none of them justifying the catastrophe rewarded to me. In my last 3 semesters, I had managed to score 75% easily. And now this disgrace was churning my interiors. There was no extent of what I was going through. I had no courage to tell mom & dad, but it was not tough for them to find out as I was at home. "What, the hell, do you study in college?? Guitar chords, is it??"

"Is this what we get in return from the son, who has never been denied for anything??" I could not answer back the rage. I dared not to.

They were right. It could not go this way. May be they had the right to say this now, but my heart did not pay consent when they even blamed music for this massacre of hopes. Music can't be a fly in the ointment of success for any one. It is an inspiration in itself. I saw an incoming call on my cell phone from Pulkit. I had already seen that he had managed to score a decent 72%. I did not want to congratulate someone when I had screwed up myself, so badly.

Moreover, I knew if I pick up the phone, mom would ask about his result. And I would not want to say "He scored 72percent in the exam that made me flunk." Her reaction on hearing that would kill me silently. Parents like making comparisons, only when their own children are on the losing end.

I disconnected the phone & switched it off. I did not feel like talking to anyone. Even more than mom's words, dad's silence pinched me. I packed my guitar & the newly acquired drums & placed them in the storeroom. I locked its door.

The day that followed was Sunday. In a way, it was good. I did not want to go to college. But I did not want to stay back. I just wanted to run away. I was almost 20 and I had never failed in one exam before.

I had often consoled many friends, not to lose heart in such a situation. But saying is easy, only saying is. Even in the darkest moment, I thought of ending it up at once. But the very next second, my family came to my mind. I had already hurt them before, they did not deserve this. I just could not ruin it for them anymore.

On Monday's morning, I wanted not to go to college. But, I had no strength to look in to my parent's eyes. So, I left for the college. Even on the way, I thought of skipping it. But, for how long could I sit back & sulk??

I went to the college, thinking that I had to return there one day or the other. Inside the college, the ambiance was pretty normal. For the first time in 2.5 years, I reached my classroom before anyone else. Very few asked me about the result. Only 2-3. I assumed the rest already knew what I was up to. But when was I correct?? People did not ask me, because then they'll have to tell me their score too. There was a mass supplementary in MICROPROCESSOR & INTERFACING. Around 35 students out of 60 had failed.

Even though, I could not go & announce this at home, but it deceased my mourning. Failure anyways means a failure. But there's a bigger truth- nothing heals like time. It heals everything that makes you suffer. To my relief, situation at home was getting normal. In college, everyone's state was alike, except some big-headed geniuses. Consequently, I started attending all the lectures. I did not roam out, to save myself from the embarrassment that I had to face after disclosing my results to anyone.

I used to pass through the corridors only twice in a day. From college gate to our block in the morning and the way back after dispersal. I was coming home one day, when unfortunately Sirat struck me. As always, she had finally appeared from nowhere. I thought, I would say a "hii" & escape down from there, before she asked about anything else. About my results!

She had made it her mind that I was a studious guy. She had even admitted this, once I came across her in the corridors. I did not want my impression to get faded and being snubbed as a 'dumb failure'. It had always been bothering me.

"Hii." she said, before I did.

"Hii." I said & acted like I needed to rush up.

"Is there something wrong??"

"No. Seems like that??" I asked, unmindfully.

"Sort of."

"Nopes." I said, straight away. And then added, "I need to leave, dear. I'll catch up later."

"Sure."

"Please don't mind that, Bye, take care."

"You too. And don't worry, some exams in life have a re-appear option too. "She said.

I left the next second, without giving a thought. I was happy she did not ask me anything. But, wait a minute. The last sentence she spoke?? What did she mean?? I'm sure if I would have been out of my mind not to understand when she spoke the last line. May be, she already knew about my results. Whatever!

Internal exams appeared up soon. I had a bigger reason to score well this time. It's amazing to see how your perspective about everything around you, changes after just one setback. I worked as hard as I could. And it got paid. I scored well in almost all the subjects.

My performance not only pulled me out of the miserable post-failure phase, but also helped a lot to improve the condition at home. Everything rolled on to usual. I was relieved that it did. Though I never told anyone, there was a void in my life. Day & night, I missed my keyboard and Guitar. Every time I looked at mom & dad, I thought of asking if I could get my necessities back. But the fear of getting a blunt 'no' pulled me back.

After a couple of days, when I found them immensely happy, since one of my cousin's marriage has got fixed. I roasted the opportunity to my own benefit. Initially, they said a 'no', but I knew they could not deny me for long. They agreed when I convinced them a lil. I promised them about not letting music affect my academic performance.

I got my guitar & keyboard, from the store-room. Holding each of them in my hands after more than three weeks, I realized how much they meant to me. More than ever before, I valued them even more now. My most prized possessions!

Arpit called me once to ask about the drums & practice. I told him that I had bought them, but I could not show a green signal for practice. I did not want another black-out at home again. So, I asked him to wait till the post-semester vacations.

The final practical's started & the semester exams began sooner for the 5th semester. I was asked by my family to put music on hold & restrict myself to the course books. It was an order, so I had no other option. I did as they asked me to. The last I wanted was disappointing them by earning another stain on my degree. My concentration was on exams & nothing else. By god's grace, exams went off really well.

The sixth semester started on 2nd February. Quite earlier than the usual! In a way, it was good for us. The college fest was meant to be organized by March's next extreme, so I was happy to get more time for the preparations. Formulating a music band was not a silk cake walk. It needed time & patience.

Not wasting much of the time, I met Arpit as soon as I could.

"Yeah, but we had just made a plan. And performing on the stage is a completely different thing, Aryan."

"It is, for sure. But everything needs a start. This might be ours. Just make one thing clear, are you willing to play??" I told him.

"I'm, indeed. But you should have consulted me once, before buying the drums. Buddy, I can't pay Rs.5000 right now." Arpit grumbled.

"Oh so that is the case. Look, I have not asked you to pay me at this moment. I'm not running anywhere, neither are you. "

"Hmmm. But I'm not that skilled, man. The entire college will be in front of us, noticing every move of ours. "

"That's what we want at the end of the day. Don't we??" I said as he nodded.

"If we practice, we can improve. We all can." I continued, trying to instill some confidence in him.

"Yup. But still...!"

"Don't worry. We'll cope-up with everything.... together. " I assured him.

"Crap it, shit shit..!" I jumped out of the car, after hearing a collapsing sound. To my fear, it was the sound of the smash between the left back light and the college's boundary wall. The back light had smeared into pieces of broken glass. It was around 6 in the wintry evening. And if you're scratching your head wondering what I was doing there, the answer is: I was returning home after putting the drums in Arpit's hostel room. But when did life plan to become easy for me?

There I was, stuck like another day, staring at the pieces of broken class which formed the back light of the car 2 minutes back. I looked around to check if anyone noticed. I could not spot anyone known outside the college. Thank god, I whispered. But the very next moment, god proved two things:

One, I was wrong.

Two, god did not deserve any 'thanks'.

My heartbeat raced up as somebody tapped at my shoulder. I turned around to find Sirat. Hats off, Mr. fate. If there was someone who could get listed amongst people making unexpected appearances at all weirdly awkward situations, it had to be undoubtedly her.

"You?? What have you been doing here??" I asked her angrily, in reflex. She was not expected to be there in that dark. The next moment, I hoped that my statement did not make me look protective about her.

"Sir, I should be the one asking this. I'm returning from home. If there is anyone whose presence needs to be questioned, it is you." she said. I thought of something to tell her, as she added, "Not willing to go home??"

"No nothing, some private work at college." I said, hoping she had not spotted me, putting a stain on my dad's prized possession. May be she had not.

"Ohoho. So by 'Private work', Mr. Aryan means bumping his car into the college building." she said, clearing all my doubts & laughed aloud. Was it even funny?? Not to me, certainly.

"So you saw it, right? Then why pretended like you did not?" I grumbled.

"Because I thought you might confess that. But how could you do that with annoying strange lass. Isn't it??" She taunted.

In no sense, I was going to explain her on 'how important she is', when I was already messed up.

"I would have, if that helped. It just happened. I left the clutch abruptly while driving back."

"Uhm, one can see well. I need to walk back. But anyways be ready..." Before she could complete, her cell-phone rang. So, she moved away. I did not speak as she has gestured me not to. So, she started moving towards the college gate. She waved bye, but I did not speak as she has gestured me not to. By the time she hung up the phone, she was already meters away from me.

"Be ready for what, ma'am?" I asked her as she hung up.

"For what your dad will do to his son." She said, turning back for a moment & disappeared. Huh. Over smart girl, I murmured to myself. .

Not Again..!

By now, I had three people prepared in my team. The drummer- assumingly. The guitarist- yes. And I- more than anyone else.

We had sought the permission for practice after the college timings. I could play guitar, but only to an extent. However, my long relationship with keyboard had taught me enough to look fair with it. So, I opted to play keyboard at the stage.

No matter how, our practice trials started. But of course, the basic necessity was yet to be fulfilled. The pivot of the band, the vocalist was still missing. And I could not shut my eyes to the fact that finding the voice of our band was the absolute need of the hour.

We had put up notices on every notice-board of our college. Whichever may be the College, Cafeteria always accounts to be the most flooded place, visited by maximum number of students. Keeping that in mind, I had converted half-a-chart into the notice highlighting our probe, for cafeteria's notice board, all by myself, quite unexpected from someone who hadn't even picked up a sketch pen ever in his drawing class. Passion has the power to make you do things, you never did before, I guess.

We had set a date for auditioning the interested ones, if any. Owing to my impatient nature, I wanted it to be as early as possible. But Arpit insisted that we should give appropriate amount of time to the students to know, think, and decide.

At the auditions, the day turned out to be a fateful one. We received good response and variety of options. 9 people came up for the auditions. Though most of the candidates preferred Hindi songs, some sang English songs. Even 2 guys, amongst those who turned up, could rap. Some of them were really OK. Some were a bit lacking by our parameters.

But we succeeded in finding someone eligible, quenching our band's thirst, Sameer. His superfluous voice made us choose him over his "not-yo-yo" type looks. We were not judging a beauty pageant after all, the 3 of us knew.

However, the drummer had a craze about growing extra-long hair, and matched them up with the weirdest kind of beard any one ever chose to keep. No one in our band could claim to look like a rockstar. Yes, we did not even possess the kind of faces only a mother can love, but we all managed to look fine. Good music does not come with the compulsion of particular looks, thankfully.

So target 1 was achieved. I had found all my “Anmol Ratna's”. We could hit the practice ground now.

We had started practice on the very next day. I had arranged the mike and amplifier from a choir. Out of the four of us, Sameer & Jatin were junior to Arpit & me. My past experience had shown me well how hierarchy could contribute in ruining peace between the members. So, I had borne in my mind to take special care that nobody felt abandoned in any sense. I battled for one more thing -If my band-mates would support my choice of playing keyboard. They did. I could give bass & lead both, through my new keyboard.

We had chosen a song by everyone's consent. Not only it was a mood setter, its scale suited Sameer's voice perfectly. I was with Jatin once, when I asked him, “You really think an acoustic guitar can work. I mean it's just a beginner's guitar, you know. ”

“Sort of, but it will. I've seen many people performing with this only.” He said.

“Of course, let's see.” He had won the talent hunt last year. So he definitely knew more about the Guitaring, I thought.

With further practice, things started taking a turn around. When we practiced, we realized the scale or volume of the guitar was somewhat low or possibly, the beat of the drum was too high, loud enough to suppress the tune of the guitar. We tried practicing for another 3 and half hours. But all in vain.

I spoke up, "wait wait. Everyone, hold on. I think we should concentrate on the Guitar. It is not properly audible. "

"Exactly. Aryan, did not you suggest Jatin to get the amplifier? One amp is just not sufficient for keyboard, guitars and mike." Arpit said and turned towards Jatin "They'll really help in raising the power." Jatin did not speak.

"It would not be easy to work without them." Arpit spoke again.

"Hmm. I agree. See Jatin, you have seen it yourself. You can reconsider the amplifier, once again." I suggested him.

"Well, I think guitar is the necessity here, not the amps on the stage."

"Is that the only reason stopping you from buying them??" I asked him back.

"Yes, with a couple of others, Inexplicable."

"But, you can adjust, we'll need them for the future too." Arpit said trying to convince him again. Jatin hardly showed any move. I did not want any rift to happen. So, I interrupted in between. We decided to call off the practice for the next day.

Inside, I was optimistic that I won't let the absence of some amplifiers to become any ordeal in my dream. I was confident that we might do it without the amps too.

On the next session of practice, Sameer turned out to be in order. He had to sing along the sync of the instruments.

"Can you sing the song without any one of us playing??" Arpit asked him.

"Like without any rhythm or beats??" Sameer said.

"Yes dear. Just like humming. It might help us. Don't worry there is no sword hanging over your head." I said. He sang the song for us and honestly, he did complete justice to the song.

"Alright then, here we go and start up together." I said, smiling at him. How contented I felt when I heard him. His voice had filled the practice room with an unusual radiance.

After a while, Sameer turned up to the Arpit and said, "Sir, I think the sound of the drums is too high. Can u beat them a little slower??"

"Of course!"

He continued to sing again. But the beat of the drums got louder than before.

"Play a bit softly." He signaled again to Arpit.

"I'm doing it from a while." Arpit replied. We jumped back to the practice. After half an hour, all of a sudden the Arpit stopped playing and stepped out from there.

"You were right, man. This beat is too frantic." He said calmly but his face was red, I observed, indicating a sense of tension.

"Hey, hey, sit buddy. Don't worry." I tried to make him comfortable as Jatin passed him some water to drink.

"I may be playing awful." He said to me worriedly and then looked at Sameer.

"That's not true, sir. Really, that isn't." Sameer answered to him starkly.

"He's right, Arpit. We are all trying hard to improve." I said.

"Hmmm, can we jam tomorrow if you don't mind? It's too late." Arpit asked.

"Yup. It's close to 11. I should go home too. We'll catch up tomorrow." I said and then turned towards Jatin.

"Can we meet tomorrow if you have a free lecture. I have some guitar-related queries, Sirrrrrr!!" I said, making a childlike innocent face.

"Ahh!! I'll let you know if I have one. But I can't promise anything." He said in a tone that only the cruelest teacher can possess. I pouted.

"Oho. Stop making faces like that. I'll call you." He said & we laughed. So did Arpit & Sameer.

We practiced for 4-5 days & continued trying to fall in synchronization with each other. For me, it had become a routine to attend college, go back home for an hour or two & then return back again for the practice sessions. It is amazing how we all get used to the joyful things in life. The practice timings were the part of the day which I used to eagerly wait for.

The four of us were practicing that night, when Sameer told Arpit politely that he was missing the beats. But Arpit seemed quite occupied.

We continued somehow, until the Sameer went a bit annoyed with Arpit and said "sir, I just told you something. And we can, at least, expect you to concentrate and follow."

I hoped the Arpit would now concentrate & improve to play the beats carefully. But he did not pay any heed and rather, he behaved in a very blatant manner.

"You better concentrate on your singing, Mr. Vocalist." he suspended Sameer off. In return, Sameer kept staring him.

I intervened. "Arpit, it happens buddy. Some beats are getting missed." Luckily, my intervention helped the situation to get calmer.

Arpit & I decided to listen to the original version of the song again, so that we could trace out the missing beats. Unlike before, Arpit gave proper attention before playing. He tried harder & harder, but it was not working at all. I hoped it would do. But it just did not. In the end, he gave up.

"Crap! What the hell am I doing here, if I can't even rattle this stupid drum??" He said clamorously. It seemed as if he had posed that question to himself. He threw away the beating sticks & ran away, towards the door.

Not again, I thought to myself. I could not let anything go wrong, splitting this band into nuggets.

I ran after him. Rest of the two followed. I stopped Arpit by his arm forcefully.

"What happened, man, all of a sudden??"

"Aryan, you are asking me 'what happened.'?? Can't you just see?? "

"See what?? Tell me what is wrong. Did anybody say something wrong to you??" I asked him patiently. He did not answer any thing &

rather tried to release his arm that I held. I budged him to speak but he did not.

"You owe me an answer goddammit. You can't leave like this. Are you listening to me?? " I shouted at him for the first time.

"Fine then, I'm tired of bearing all this. I can't handle it anymore." I expected him to speak out whatever he had in his head but he did not & became silent again. I realized I had to evoke him again.

"What does 'it' mean?? Speak up for yourself man. What is bothering you so much??"

"This criticism. I can barely see you guys playing so well. I'm just spoiling things, driving them to the worst. I had told you earlier that I might not be able to match up with you guys. Then why, why did you involve me??"

"There is no point in brooding. I know you had made yourself clear. But I also told you that things can take a better turn. This is a chance for all of us." I said

"Whatever it is. But I just want to get out of this shit." What so ever he said, he raised my heckles.

"Then fuck off." I screamed and left the place.

How else do I answer a guy who called my dream crap? That was the first time in life that I used such a word. Even when I said it, I was sure that it would not be possible for us to perform anything together.

But Jatin & Sameer's convincing power made the impossible happen. They brought us together at least for once. However, it proved to be another fiasco. Even after we gave up our ego, we could not carry on for too long. There was hardly any spot of compatibility & coordination between us. We gave up just a week before the college fest.

2 days later, I decided to lock up the place where we used to practice. It was hardly of any avail to me now, so I went to return back the keys to the ma'am-in-charge. Spotting any professor in the college premises except the lecture hall is no less than a tedious task. Finally, half a round of the whole college made me find the needed of the

“endangered” species. She was involved in a decoration team. I returned back the keys, avoiding any large conversations.

The moment I turned to march back, Sirat was standing in front of me, with her trademark cheesy smile.

She said “Hiiiiii.” Her ‘Hiii’ was as cheesier as she was.

“Hii.” I replied & kept it short.

“What happened?? Did you just proposed someone & got spanked in the return?? ” she said and chuckled. I gave her a disgusted look, my trademark, enough to make her realize that I was in nooooo mood to appreciate her self-entertaining jokes.

“Oh. I think I’m sorry.”

“That’s OK. May I leave??” I asked her started moving away without her consent. Must have been rude of me. But thank god!

I had taken just a few steps, when I realized something. She had been running slowly towards me & had reached me almost. “Sir, Sir, Sir. Would you mind if I take two minutes of yours??”

I did not rebel. “OK sure.” I said.

“I just wanted to say ‘thanks’ to you for the book you lent to me. I know it’s stupid of me saying it after a long time.”

“Never mind. You’re welcome”

“Hmmm. But not like this.” she said sheepishly.

“Then like what?” She offered some chocolates to me.

“Oh thank you. But I don’t like chocolates. ”

“Realllllllllllllllllyy??” she said it over dramatically, making me wonder as if I had said no to “oxygen.”

“But they are good for health.”

“Oh reallllllly” I said imitating her. “So who discovered this fact?? Ms. Sirat??”

“No. But seriously, they are good. Do you know people who eat chocolates can survive more than those who do not??”

"In that case, you are immortal." I said

"Shhh!! How did you just find out my secret?? Please don't tell it to anyone." She whispered.

"Sorry. Won't be able to help much in this." I teased back.

She pouted. I said "wait let me see. Actually I can, if."

"If what?????"

"If I get two of them" I said, winking & pointed towards the chocolates. She gave them to me & said, "But only 1 condition, if we can share them." How much did she love chocolates? We shared them.

I was not exactly in a really joyful mood, but I was feeling much better. Then she asked me something which I did not expect her to. She asked "So, why are you upset??"

"Am I?? Are you kidding me??"

"No not kidding this time." Her expressions were rarely serious, but at that moment, to hell, they were.

"It is something related to the music band. It did kind of split up, no??" She answered her own question.

"It never got formed." I said.

"But what happened??"

I kept mum. "It is OK. I should not be intruding so much, being an outsider" She said.

"No no, it is not like that. Actually due to a variety of reasons, we could not fall into the proper sync."

"But you play well. I had noticed it in our fresher's party" she added. "And I'm sure the rest of your band members must be equally competitive."

"They are. We do possess some talent. But formulating a band is not as simple as that. It is not an individual performance. And many other things are to be taken into consideration." She listened with concentration, looking in to my eyes. I moved away mine. "So we tried hard, but it just did not work."

"Hmmm." she said, lost in her thoughts.

"But it happens in life. May be another time. We'll try in the next year fest. The worst part is that though I don't have any option right now, but I want to perform at any cost."

"At any cost, right??" She asked as I said a "Yes."

"Sir, if you don't mind may I suggest something?" I nodded.

"You don't realize but you actually have an option. You can ask for a position in the 'Vishesh'. Who would not like to have a good keyboard player by their side??"

"Vishesh??" I said, trying to hide my grim & wondering at such an idea. In one word, it was irrelevant!

"Yes. But is there something wrong about them??" She had caught me again.

"No."

"You're not meant to hide things. Actually I thought some of them are your classmates. So it might be helpful. "

"Yeah right. They and help?? Just the way they did a year ago." I tried to wrap up & change the topic. But who could hide things from Ms. Detective. I told her everything.

"So how can I go & ask them now? Tell me."

She thought for a lil while and said, "You said that you wanted to perform at any cost. May be a phone call is that cost. You can just let them know that you are interested. Rest is their choice. And we both know getting a positive response can mend everything." She was so unbeatable in pushing someone. After a minute, she received a call.

"Oh no. I did not realize I'm so dead late. I just need to reach for my practice in the mechanical block." She exclaimed the moment she hung up the phone.

"Rescue finally, thank god." I laughed. She pouted.

"I was kidding mam. Alright I'll walk you there." I said. She smiled. Till we both reached the venue, she had given me some more 'convincible' tips. Before she left, she asked me for a final decision if I could call them or not.

"I will but conditions apply." I said.

"And that means."

"That I'll not share my chocolates with you." I said and laughed.

"Not possible. Well, in that case, you can forget about the call. " She said teasingly and we laughed harder. I waved her good-bye.

Later that eve, I picked up my phone, opened up the contact list, found Ameesh's number and pressed the cancel button. I was totally confused. I wanted to call him up, but my ego held me back. It was not that easy for me to forget everything in one flash. But I recalled what Sirat said during the day. After 20 minutes of striving, I managed to press the 'call' button, instead of 'cancel'.

"Hello." it was Ameesh's voice. I could recognize it since we were friends at some point of time in the past, or at least I thought we were.

"Hii, Aryan here." I said. It was hesitating for anyone to speak up to someone, you never wanted to. A huge chunk of ego needs to be given up for letting that happen.

"Ahh yes. I have your contact number. So, how have you been??"

"I'm pretty fine. So preparing for the fest??" I could hear the noise behind him, so it was not tough to make out that they were jamming.

"Exactly. You tell me what are you up to?? How come you remember me??"

"Actually, I needed to talk to you about something important."

He listened quietly. Gathering all my courage, I finally spoke up, "Since I knew you guys would be performing, so I thought if I could .... be a part of it. I mean if I can play keyboard with you guys??"

He thought for a while. Unfortunately, conversing over the phone, I could not see his expressions.

"Do you mean with 'Vishesh'??" Of course, I meant 'Vishesh', what else could I be talking about to him.

"Yes, I hope you can help me in this." I said. I could have added 'being a friend of mine' in my statement, but I did not. One of things I hate most is 'Exaggeration'.

"Oh I see. Actually Aryan I need to discuss about this with the rest of the members. I can't promise anything on my own & despair you later." He said.

"Of course. I'll be waiting keenly."

"OK. I'll let you know then."

"By the way, buddy please try & convince them."

"I will, for sure. Listen dear, I've got to go now."

"OK. Bye."

"Bye" he said & hung up the phone.

I felt relieved, but at the same time I was tensed too. Relieved because I had solved my dilemma. Tensed because I did not know what the answer would be. I wanted it to be a 'yes' desperately. I could not sleep a wink that night. Dreams of performing in front of the whole college had replaced the slumber in my eyes.

I wanted to call up Ameesh in the morning itself. But I did not want to reveal my nervousness to anyone. I waited till the afternoon. When the afternoon arrived, I told myself that evening would be a better time.

I called him up at 5:30 pm. He picked up the phone. After a petite chat, I asked him for the answer I was waiting to know.

"You said you people will discuss if I can join you."

"Oh yes. I remember. I'm really afraid to say we got too busy last night. The schedule is really very hectic." He said evasively. He did not answer the question that I had asked him.

"So should I understand that you did not disclose the matter to them??'

“No no. I have told them that you have offered. And we were about to discuss about it. But you know these are busy days. Anyways be patient, Aryan. I’ll call you myself this time just as we take a decision.” He said consolingly.

“Hmmm. Actually it’s only 5 days left for the fest, so I thought if you all could do it at the earliest.”

“Yes, yes. I do understand your concern. I’ll call you quickly. Do wait for it. ” With that, we hung up the phone.

I waited for his call for a couple of minutes. Minutes shortly converted into hours. Somewhere in my heart, I was dreading of getting despair again.

Next day in the college, I saw Rohit, Vishesh’s bass guitarist, at some distance. Unlike my usual behaviour, I called out his name, the moment he crossed me in the corridors. He threw a look at me and said mildly, "Yeah."

I signaled him to stop moving and shared with him my wish to be a part of Vishesh. His expression hardly changed when I told him that. So, I asked with hope if Ameesh had discussed about it with them.

He said in sheer arrogance, "yeah, he was saying something. Aryan, he will tell you more about it.” His ‘Why-am-I-stuck-here’ expression was enough to make me realize that he deserved the kind of behaviour I have shown to him in the past year. Expecting anything polite from him was like chasing shadows. Both are a waste of time.

I said, "OK." and left the place.

I wondered if I should call Ameesh myself. May be I should. After all, I needed them much more than they needed me. But I could not afford to make a fool of myself, who is sticking to someone.

If I could meet Sirat somewhere, I thought. In my eyes, she seemed much more decisive than me, at least in that matter. But how do I find her?? I did not even have her contact number. That was the 1st time I wanted to meet her so badly. Sarcastic as life is, I could not see her.

I decided to call up Ameesh on my own.

“Hello.” He spoke.

"Hey." I said thinking what to say next.

"Yeah Aryan, tell me." He said of all possible things I had imagined him saying. How was I supposed to tell him something every time? Had he completely forgotten that he had told me that he'll call me up?

"Ameesh actually, the 1st string of my guitar has got broken. I was wondering who I could ask for an extra one. Do you possess one??" I asked him.

"I do. You can collect it from me anytime." He said. I expected him to tell me what their final verdict was. He would initiate if they want me to join or at least they'll let me know in the other case.

He spoke again, as I was expecting him to. But what he said was a bolt from the blue for me. He said "yar I need to go, they are calling for the practice. Bye. Take care." He hung up the phone very next second.

I felt like throwing away my phone at the wall facing me. But 'thanks' to Ameesh. He managed to keep up to my expectations like always. My chances of performing hinged on him, consequently they got ruined. All over again! I tried hard to test my luck, even till the last days before the fest, but all in vain, fruitlessness. I could not perform on the stage of fest 2010 too.

That year, our college had organized a techno-cultural fest. Apart from all the music-dance-and-drama, there were various technical competitions organized for the students.

Pulkit knew that I was upset, so he announced over the phone, "I am putting your name in Virus programming event, and we both are going to co-ordinate it." His love for computers & programming had never ceased to gain my attention, even much before we were friends, the way we were today.

"Man, you are well aware that I don't even have the faintest idea about Virus." I said.

"I know, but I'll make you learn whatever is required. And you just need to have a little idea". He said.

"But still. Isn't it a waste of your time?" I said, as I knew clearly that it was an attempt to perk me up.

“It is not, and I’ll manage everything. Trust me on that.”

"OK. Let’s go ahead." I said.

I was desperate to get involved & focus on something useful, rather than spending the fest in a grave manner, mourning for another crash in attempting for music.

Our team was asked to coordinate a ‘Virus programming’ competition in which the participants were supposed to make a computer programs. Though, Pulkit had taught me some concepts, but even then making a ‘virus’ was not my cup of tea. Many of the people around me were exposed to this fact as much as I was. Dramatically some of them were loose cannons. They were never nice to me and vice-verse. So they exploited every opportunity to trouble me, and raising my temperature.

Amongst them, Manav had no close competitor in pissing me off. From the very day of 2nd year’s fresher’s party, he has treated me as I had to pay back loans to him.

Time and again, I had heard about his hatred for me. His true feelings towards me revisited when he tried to get me evicted from the coordinating team.

“Why are you getting so shocked looking at me??” I went straight to Manav to get one on one. He was quite stunned to see me. He tried to conceal what he was feeling, but his expressions revealed it.

“No no. I’m completely fine. Why would I get shocked?? ” he said, sounding overprotecting. To say the least, he was a really bad actor.

“Ohh really, so I need to tell you that too. I thought you know the reason behind it. Don’t you??”

“What are you talking about, man?? Be clear.”

I kept staring into his eyes. They spoke of my anguish.

“Say something. Why are you staring me like that??” he asked me again. May be I should give voice to my thoughts.

“Listen man, stop mocking in front of me. I’m least interested in whatever you do. I have seen you intervening in my ways even before, but I'm in no mood to ignore & bear all these creepy things" I told him pointing towards his face.

"Ohh but what makes you think all this. See, I have better things to do in life rather than just enticing you."

"We all are supposed to be aware of how much of that statement is valid. What makes you think that you can go to the organizing team last night & blabber anything about me? And I'll sit quietly like a kid playing with his cradle. Who are you to make any remark about me?" I said.

He kept mum. I was at the top of disgruntlement by now. "So better stay out of my things or I'll not yield you any good I promise." I threatened him. Pulkit, who stood behind me, had realized that I was getting too angry. So he had to get me controlled. So he tried to pacify the situation & pulled me out of the heated up scene. I did not resist much since I had already made clear what my point was.

It hurts only when!!

On the day of the 'Virus programming' competition, I gaily reached the college to report on time. I was happy, praising myself, in my mind that I had fought over the hurdles, and had ruined all contemplations plotted against me. But what after that??????

The event began at 10:30 a.m. While the participating teams were trying to make viruses, I was hovering around with my companions, keeping an eye on the participants so that no one peeks into the other team's monitor. The labs have been divided so I had two people with me, Pulkit of course, and Karan, another who was chosen for the task. Both of them were intelligent guys, and were familiar with me.

"Excuse me sir." A team called me. It was not time for teams to wrap up, so I went confidently towards them. I was really certain because I thought they would not have finished the tough task that sooner. "Yeah tell me." I said sounding like a connoisseur of programming.

"Sir we have completed our project, you can check it out." I stayed in awe.

How come 'so soon'? I mean yes, I was not supposed to make silly puzzled expressions, glancing at the faces and at their monitor's screen, but to check it. But how could I?? I had never made a virus myself ever. Though I had tried it, but gave up the idea. And how these super intelligent–super confident devils could choose me of all the 3? I wondered if they were some distant relatives of Manav. I asked if they were sure. Of course they were. Something clicked in my mind.

"Karan, will you come here, please??" I asked Karan.

Not only intelligent, he was even an obedient down to earth kind of a guy. I asked him to check the query, making an excuse that I had to make a really urgent call. Cell-phones have made life, for sure, easier. What else does serve as an excuse that works 9 out of 10 times?

Karan accepted very excitedly as if he was dying to offer his brain some exercise. I came out of the lab as fast as I could, rescuing myself. So when I was out there, enjoying the things around me and wondering what to do, I saw Sirat.

Hush!! This girl meets me at all unexpected times. But days before, when I was praying to see her desperately, it seemed as if she had gone to hibernate in a molehill.

"Oh Hii."

"Hii, Out of breath. Are you going to catch a flight??" she asked. Yes, I was breathing faster since I had just escaped out of the block.

"No no actually, I'm a part of the 'programming team', so pretty occupied with that work."

"Oh I can see that really well" she said taunting at me, rolling her eyes.

"You picked me wrong, Ma'am. I just came here to get some fresh air." I said, hoping she would believe me.

"Don't worry sir, I won't complain against you." She winked & smiled.

"Hahaha, well that would be so kind of you." I said.

And then I narrated the story of my narrow flee from the geeks who were passionate about making computer virus. She laughed. "Hey, are you laughing at me? Don't forget I am senior to you." I said, teasing her.

"Hmmm." She said and burst out laughing again. "Tell me. Is there any progress with 'Vishesh'?"

"I called them that same evening."

"SOOO? What did they say???? " She asked me, light in her eyes reflected, making them shine.

"They fired me, even before the recruitment." I said & laughed. But she did not.

I tried to change the topic. “Don’t worry, expecting them to help me is next to building castles in the air. Tell me girl, what is up about your practice?? Announcing this time too no??” I asked her.

“Yeah I’m. And it is going good. After all, it is the only thing I’m doing from years.”

“One can guess it easily; you are really good at it.” I said.

“Ohh, am I??”

“Yes. And I’m not kidding.” I said, assuring her.

“Well in that case thanks, sir.” She smiled to me. Her smile was contagious.

“You’re welcome. I think I should go back now, the checking stuff would have got over by now.” I said, winking.

She nodded and then said, “Did nobody tell you??”

“Tell me what??”

“That you are so mean...” she said, stretching the ‘mean’ too long.

“Seriously??”

“Yes. So mean..........ingly vivacious.” She said, winked at her tactfulness and we both laughed again.

I joined them back, marked my ‘present’, the reason behind my returning there. Not a surprise, Pulkit looked ready to blurt out his frustration for my disappearance amid. But I gave stretched explanations to coax him the very moment we stepped out. We collected the coordinators’ certificates the following week. After the fest, the internal exams took over us as always. Lectures, Labs, some more lectures, and some more Labs.

In the 2nd week of April, I received a letter addressed for me. It was the re-evaluation result. When I applied for the re-evaluation, I was quite confident. I had a gut feeling that this time I would get a green signal in the ‘microprocessors & interface’ exam. Though none of my wishes got processed at all and I hinged on the interface of failure again. I did not get clear this time too. May be, it would take me some more time to get rid of this stain on my mark-sheet, I thought to myself.

Meanwhile all this, my interaction with Sirat inflated. And she became a friend, a friend who had all the stupid qualities in this world that a human being can possess.

We'd exchanged contact numbers purely due to academically useful reasons. She said that she wanted to ask for some queries regarding one of the subjects.

"Don't worry. I would not bother you by giving blank calls day & night." She tried to assure me and make fun at the same time.

"That does not seem possible as much as I know you." I teased her back.

But she did not step back from her words & asked me only about study-related things over the text messages. Sometimes, I would drop a forwarded message in her inbox. She too started doing the same. She called me once to wish Good day. Quite unsurprisingly, we kept talking & talking & hung the phone after 27 minutes.

Semester exams approached. I knew I had one more thing to accomplish- the 'microprocessor.' exam. How difficult it seems to study the same book all over again for clearing a supplementary. But I could not afford to take a chance this time. So I chose to study it hard. All the exams went off well. Yes, all of them.

Sitting with juniors during the Microprocessor's exam, it felt really awkward. And, I tried ignoring whenever any known junior came around me. However since, there were many of my classmates, the embarrassment decreased gradually. And thank god, it went nice.

The semester was done, so now it was time for the 3rd year training. My rendezvous with Chandigarh had taught me an indispensable lesson that there's no place like home. Staying at home & working on your own can be much more improvising than roaming motivelessly in institutions. So I decided to take up the training in Kurukshetra itself, which meant I could traverse down there for one hour & come back just after the class. It helped me a lot in utilizing my time for music properly. And to be honest, I was much more devoted towards my training than I was the last time. I can proudly say that I made those 45 days quite productive in real sense.

We joined back the college on 15th September. The 4th year had begun, the final year of my engineering studies. The past 3 years had taught me enough to play cool by now. I did not drag things when chucking them off was easy. I had begun to enjoy the pleasure of sitting on the back benches, quite contrary to my favourite spot in the 1st two years of my engineering, the front rows.

I was trying hard to make guitar a charm of my hands. Fortunately, I had succeeded in getting familiar with the six strings. So, I could hold my head high and announce to myself that MUSIC was in action. There was one thing more that demanded equal attention from me was my job placement. I was in the final year & at this stage not paying any heed to recruitment could be the best way to bully one-self. So I made up my mind to concentrate on it all along, even though it was four months away.

Somehow, it had become habitual for me to talk to the 'kiddish' girl, as I used to call her teasingly. Meanwhile, many people, who I bothered about or not, were busy pondering over my craving to form a music band. Uninvited criticism was a gift that I was endowed with, that too in abundance. It did not hurt me. Dogs bark any way. Those lampoons wanted me to give up, but I did not.

But what affected me was when my best friend Pulkit ended up saying one day, "You still want to do this??"

"I did not get what you mean."

He thought for a while and then spoke the most unpleasant line he could ever say, "The music band and all, yaar. Look Aryan, you've wasted considerable amount of your time and hardly earned anything till now."

The world had blacked out for me on hearing it from his mouth, as he continued "And what if you even succeed now, it's the last year Aryan, no one would remember that you ever made a band."

I kept quiet. May be he took my silence as my resignation. I did not get infuriated at him, because his concern for me was making him speak the pits. But I was hurt and disappointed. What I knew was just that I was in no state to step back. Doing that is no less than insanity, especially when you have set your heart on that thing for that long.

I wanted to talk to someone, somebody who would not be as disheartening as everybody else. During this time, Sirat and I started exchanging messages, she would often send me something answerable. 'Choose one & I'll tell you this' kind of stuff and we would start chatting.

I called up Sirat for the 1st time myself.

"Hello." She said as she picked up the phone.

"Hello." I tried to sound normal.

"Hi how are you?"

"I'm pretty good, u tell me how are you?"

"Sir, I'm confused."

"Confused regarding what??"

"That should I propose you or not." She said and busted out laughing.

I wondered if that was a joke.

"Whatever." I said. But she clarified herself saying she was kidding.

"Actually, I'm confused about the reason that is making you sound so low??"

"Really? Do I?"

"Of course you are. And your victorious 'Do-I' is not working this time. You can tell me what is it?"

I was quite again, which was enough for her to realize that it was not the right moment. It was not that I did not want to tell her. But the question was how??

She flipped on to something else. "So tell me something what is happening around?"

"I'm just at home. Waiting for my dinner, Mum is cooking may be." I said half-heartedly.

"Wow, you made me skip a beat. I mean home & the food. "

"Hmmm. So, do you miss your home??"

"A LOT..! I mean more than anything else. In fact, I was just planning to go back home the upcoming weekend. But 2 days would not be enough. I would kill most of the time on the way itself. " She sounded disappointed, of course a way less disappointed than I was.

"Hmmm. So where do you belong to?" I asked her, not to run out of the conversation.

"Delhi. And by the way, you don't even know this." She said complaining the very next moment.

"I'm sorry. I did not know the mental asylum got shifted from Agra to Delhi. Otherwise, I would not have asked this. By the way, when did it shift? " I laughed harder. So did her.

"Ohh so Delhi girl, hmm. That makes me think I should stay away from you. I have heard they are a real trap." I continued teasing.

"Real trap? Huh, as if you're that naïve!"

Finally I told her about the non-gracious comments that I got to listen. She listened very patiently when I told her all this. There was something nice about her. She knew when not to crack jokes.

After talking to her, there was one thing clear in my mind. Criticism by your closest ones can be of great use sometimes. You may hate them for the critics at that moment but it can make you spurs on heights, more than anything else. I wanted to make my desire come alive; I knew I had to pull up my socks for this. It was the last chance for me to prove I was right, and others were not.

2 weeks later:

I was confident this year that I could manage to play guitar on the stage now. Moreover, I was pushed to try harder than ever before. So, I was determined to get us all together again.
I did not know whom to start with. I was a bit subtle to call the Arpit. But I had to, since he was a really important necessity for the band, plus he would require much more time to pick up than the rest of us. I was aware of this in my hearts of hearts. I called him up.

"Hello." He said.

"Hello. How are you??"

"I am fine dude. I was just thinking about you."

"About me? Hey wait wait, man I am not that way." I said & laughed at him.

"Shut up man, neither am I. And you dare not suspect about it. Actually, I was thinking about the fest. Our performance. "

"The music band??" I asked him.

"That's it. I think we should reunite & try again if you agree." He said. Oh god, was he reading my mind so that he could say all this?

"Agree??"

He interrupted before I could say anything and said "yes. And I have made up some balance too for paying you back the cost of the drums, like we discussed before. May I buy them from you??"

I felt like jumping on the sofa I was sitting at.

"Yeah. But are you sure that you want to?"

"Hmmm, I'm. But you are the pivot, man. Don't say no."

"No?? Dear, I swear I just called you to ask about our take on the reunion and you just stole my words. That's so unbelievable. " I told him.

I sold him the drums for Rs. 3500. The loss of a few hundred made me earn an invaluable profit. He looked so sure & interested unlike the last time. I made him promise that he'll practice them from then onwards.

Once a while, I have to go to the college at 7 in the evening to borrow a book from a friend of mine. I am passing from the corridor of boys' hostel when I see 3-4 guys practicing with their instruments. It is 'Vishesh', so I try not to go close and make a distance from them.

Suddenly, my gaze falls on one of those guys and I take step aback. It is tough to understand his presence there. He is neither Ameesh, nor Rohit. He is Jatin. But was not he on my side?

Yes, he was but only till the moment I saw him with them. On my way back to home, I realize why could make him turn back at us. I understand why he has been in a 'no-message-no-call' genre from so many days. Of course why would he need to acknowledge me now, realizing I am of least benefit to him by now.

'Vishesh' required a guitarist we had heard from the starting days of 7th semester, ever since their Tushar, Vishal and Sandy had completed their degree and bid an adieu to the college & their band. Their requirement must have got fulfilled in form of Jatin. Of course like others, he too has deemed that we would never get succeeded. And accepting him would have overjoyed Ameesh & Rohit, because it will pinch me to lose him. I decide to consider the Jatin a bygone from then. It is also the day when I took the stand of buying an electric guitar.

After the internal exams, one day I met someone. He was a guy with typical blonde hair. Something we don't find very usually in place like ours. He came up to me & shook hand with me. My confused expression spoke for me & it said "Do I know you??" My memory had never been a good friend of mine.

"Sir, I am Ajit, you did not recognize me."

I tried hard to do so, but it could not. All that I could make up was that I have seen this face earlier.

"Sir, you auditioned for a vocalist last year." I nodded. "I was one amongst the guys. I did a rap." He said, finally helping my 'tube-light' brain to glow up.

"Oh yeah. So here I remember. I'm really sorry. "

"Oh c'mon sir. It's ok. I wanted to know if you are forming up a band this time."

Tough question to answer, it was. Of course, I wanted to, but the only doubt was..... Actually everything, except my will, was a big question mark for me.

"Yeah. We'll try up again I suppose. We will." I articulated, hoping each word of my statement comes true.

"Sir, if you don't mind may I ask something?"

"Go ahead." I smiled at him.

"Actually I was thinking if I could try and join your band. I have even brought an electric guitar and I'm trying to learn it by following video tutorials over the internet. " He said, to my utmost surprise, pushing me into a world of thoughts.

"That seems interesting I see. So, how long has it been that you are trying this way?? " I asked him.

"Around 10weeks.and I can do chord-shifting easily." He answered confidently.

Before I could say something, he said, "Sir, I'm quite awake to the fact how much you are pining for getting to do some music action on the fest stage. Just like you, I too have that desire."

There was zeal in his voice when he said that. I had made a decision in my mind, but his words made me assured that I was doing the right thing.

I went back and recalled that he had done a good job in rapping. But the reason why he was not chosen by us was it was supposed to be our 1st chance to perform. And I could not afford to gamble on it, so we'd decided to play safe. But now, a year after, my belief in conventionality had evaporated up in the air. Life is all about risks. And who knows, he may turn out to be the knight in shining armor.

"Ok. I think we can consider thinking about you as a part of the band. "

"So does that mean??" He asked impatiently.

"Yes, but I can judge only after a trail. Would you mind that?"

"Of course not." He agreed whole-heartedly.

I knew that he was a good rapper. It was something that one could easily make that out. His extra-fair skin and that sort of hair were a supplementary to his talent. I just wanted to get assured about his guitar playing abilities.

We went to his hostel room, during the lunch time next day. I asked him to play the rhythm and do some chord shifting. To my wonder, he played quite well, though there was a lot of room for improvement. But that's the way you learn it. He had even brought amplifier and Processor along with his electric guitar. So in my mind, I was determining the pros and cons of inviting him in the band. Certainly, the pros outweighed the cons.

He also introduced me to his roommate, Anshul.

"Sir, Anshul also has interest in playing guitar." Ajit told me.

"Ohh that is really nice. So can you also play like Ajit, Anshul??" I asked him.

"Not that good, sir. He is all into music. However, I do it just for enjoyment. But yes, it inspires me a lot of times. Actually when the Ajit announced that he was going to buy an electric guitar, I was at the top of excitement. "Anshul said.

"Hehe. Yeah. That even makes me remember many things. " The lunch got over and we all had to come back.

"Sir, what have you decided about me?" Ajit asked me, while we were all marching out of the boys' hostel.

"I think I will be certifiable to invite you to perform with us." I said to him on October 28th, 2010.

I was aware of what had ruined my plans and crushed my hopes the last year. So I wanted to start off the practice sessions as soon as possible this time, so that we have plenty of time to fall in perfect synchronization with each other.

Ajit and I started playing together. I gave it a thought to involve the Arpit too from day one, but then it would be a blunder to repeat the same mistake all over again. I did not want too many cook to spoil the broth, that I waiting for, from years. So I thought patiently & practically.

As we started this time, I could feel the same as I did a year before. Some things never fail to make an ignition inside you. These are actually one's true passion. But this time it was a 'do or die' situation for me. When I got tired and wanted to call off practice, I would tell myself "If not this year, it would be never again. Never Ever!" And suddenly a force would push me back again.

I received a text that eve saying the 4th semester's result was out. The very next moment I switched on my PC and logged onto the university's website. Typing my roll number, took me back to the memoirs of the past, when I logged on this site the last time. I wished today was not going to be like that scary one. As the request was being processed, different questions continued darted inside me. The questions my pounding heart was putting to my brain.

What if I get flunk this time again?? What if I had to pay for somebody else's mistake?? What if this result too proves out to be an envoy of disappointment??

As the required webpage opened up, I gathered enough courage and read what it said. It said I had got cleared. Thank god. He had finally done justice to me, by letting me down. The subject called 'Microprocessor & Interface' was no longer a hurdle in my way. I could finally sit in any interview.

A week later, I got my revised Mark sheet from the university, the one without any stains. I had scored 66 marks in 'M.I.'. It brought an equally broad smile to my face as the 1st semester's did. Of course, the thing valued the most is always the one that you have waited for the longest. With this Mark sheet, my folder of document got completed.

I was practicing along with the Ajit when his cell phone beeped. He went back to check for the message.

"Oh crap." He said the next moment, making me wonder what made him react like that.

"Did anything go wrong??" I asked him.

"I suppose." He said and passed over his cell phone to me. There was a message from Anshul which said:

'Date sheet over the net. Finals commence next Monday.'

I was taken aback. I managed to ask him "are you sure he is not trying to befool??"

"Sir, he is not that kind of a guy."

The next moment, Pulkit called me up, finally clearing all our doubts. "Yes I've checked it on the internet myself."

"That is no way man. I had so many hopes about our practice." I was pissed off.

"Hmm. Any ways where are you??" I told him I was at practice. Obviously, he did not appreciate but kept mum, in order not to contribute my already spoiled mood.

"Ok, let's see." I said & disconnected the phone. And soon to my wildest hopes, the exams appeared up in front of us, from nowhere.

When destiny plays its role!

Least to say, we had to put our practice in abeyance. It was not a decision but an imposition that we were forced to follow. I gave a thought about how to carry on our practice sessions for some days, but they were of no avail. After all, I could not afford to score a crash in the 4th year of my engineering.

The finals went really well. To me, the 4 subject's course looked like a child's play, after having to study the 6+1 subjects, last year. Finally to my resort, my last exam got finished on 6th Jan 2011. I was a man of my own wishes again, untamed.

It was almost a week after the new year, 2011's arrival bought me a good news. So now there were no exams, no supplementary, luckily. And it was time for me to get in order for recruitment. Our college usually brings 'Tata Consultancy Services' or better known as TCS in the first week of February. So I realized that I had to pull up my socks & secure a job for myself, so that I do not have to get out of this college taking home the tag of being 'idle & jobless'.

My exams had got over soon as I had just four subjects in the semester, but for Sirat, it was many yards to go. Her exams were meant to get wrapped up after 10 days.

From the day I had come across the fact that she was good in English, we had always conversed in English and I had asked her to spot grammatical errors in my language. I had also asked her once if she would help me out during my placement drills, she had promised me that she would, at any cost. And she fulfilled it when the time came.

She was a good student & had secured a presentable mark sheet for herself. So even though, I was quite confident about her performance in her own exams too, still I did not want her to ruin her degree. We were coming out of the Computers department one day, when she mocked, “Are you writing depressing poetry now-a-days??”

“Yes. How did you figure this out?” I mocked back.

“Your serious thoughtful expression told that to me.”

“Actually, I’m thinking about something important.” I said to her and added as an afterthought, “It is nice that you are still determined to assist me, but you should not avoid the fact that you still have some exams left, I mean.”

“Sir, so you want to convey that I should behave mean, and step back from my own words. And say ‘Good luck’ to you. ”

“No no, see if you do not get good marks, you come & blame me in the end, won’t you??”

“Oh, I will surely.” She tittered and then said, “I have an idea. Let’s say I have exams so I’ll study like my routine, and after finishing my target, when I march to bed, I’ll talk to you at that time. What do you say?”

I was confused to the depth, as always.

“See, I’m not sacrificing studies, but just giving up a bit of sleep. So it can work.” She said.

“I can and that’s quite thoughtful of you, ma’am.”

“Thanks. Ok, tell me something important, you have less than a month in hand. How are you going to prepare?? ”

“I have laid a schedule for it. I’ll start up with the 7th semester’s syllabus, since it is quite afresh in my mind, and then I’ll take up the 6th semester’s course, and the rest will follow after the other. ”

“That sounds like your road to success. And what about me??”

“I’m counting on you Sirat, and you are so selfish, huh! This was not what I expected from you. ” I told her dramatically.

I could see her expressions changing abruptly. She must have wondered what she had done so wrong in a split second. And then I added, “You have one complete year to go for your placements. Mine is just a month away and you are worried about yourself asking 'What about me?' " with that, I burst out laughing at the top of my lungs.

"Oh my goodness! You are just gone." She said & mocked hitting me with the book in her hand. But then managing to control her laughter, she got back, "I just wanted to know about 'how may I help you in this?'."

"Yeah, you can help." I told her absent-mindedly.

"That is what I'm asking. In what way??"

"I have thought about this too. See you can be helpful in the manner if you put tricky questions from the course of your present semester. "

"Ohh! So, that is some kind of a mock interview." Thank god, she understood.

"Exactly. And you know what! It can prove out to be a really good exercise." I told her matter-of-factly.

She nodded and asked, "Are you sure I can lend a hand??"

"Of course, but only if Ms. Interviewer knows something to ask." I ridiculed.

"And of course if Mr. Interviewee promises to give her a treat after he gets placed." She chuckled. We both smiled because both of us were waiting for it to happen.

My preparations for 'TCS' began on 13th Jan-2011. I had talked to many seniors who had got placed there, and had gathered enough information which could serve as a great aid for me to differentiate between what to do & what not to. They had even given me some tips regarding their recruitment policy. So now the mist from my eyes had got removed making me see my target.

Level 1~ the multiple choice questions test.

To prepare for the first round of my ordeal, I had brought the Aptitude books. It looked like a volcano of interrogations ready to erupt any moment, taking me in its gulp. During the day, I would study & revise the course so that nights could be employed for revisions and doubts.

It was not that much easy to get placement in TCS also I didn't want to take any chance. So mugging up from just a book was not really satisfactory. I had decided to crack the kind of questions that appear time & again. I had downloaded them from the internet. Of course, internet can serve more than just being a time-killer. There is no essence like 'internet', when put into good use. Who else could make it sound better than a potential computer engineer himself?

Though we had decided to study on our own, but Pulkit & I had settled to meet once after every week to discuss each other's doubts. We were at my place once, when we wrapped up with the queries, and enjoying tea.

He said "you know Ameesh called me two days ago."

"Did he??" I was amazed.

"Indeed. He wanted to talk about you." Now it was another time I was knocked for a six yet again.

"About me? Ahh, great!! Good going, buddy. As much as I'm enjoying this prank, chuck it. " I told him, dismissing his ridiculous sense of humour.

"I'm damn serious. It is not a hoax." He said believingly.

"Ok. So what did he say??"

"He said that he wanted your help. So he wanted me to put that in the picture before you. "

"Of course, why would he call us with any interest of his own? Ameesh was so predictable."

"Yeah, he had some university's chores pending, and your acquaintance who works there can help."

"Ohoho. So who do I look like?? Mother Teresa??"I said.

"Hehe. To him, may be you do." He giggled.

"Any ways, what did you tell him?" I enquired.

"That I'll try if I get to speak to you. So you can call him."

My eyes widened up. I told him back "Why should I call him? If he needs, he'll call me on his own."

"I am surviving in the hope that he does. It would be fun." he said.

"We are gossiping now, you know." I alarmed him. Of course, after a hiatus of time, every discussion befalls into the category of gossips.

"May be, but you better tell me the moment he call you." He said. I wondered how Pulkit could be that sure that he will.

I was busy, tormenting myself with another dose of never-ending & mind-wrecking questions, when I received a call.

Without even looking at the caller's name, I pick up the phone and say "Hello." Must be Pulkit or Sirat, I thought to myself.

"Hii, Ameesh here." He was too mild to be heard properly.

"Pardon." I said, as I checked for the name on my phone's screen.

"Ameesh, your classmate." I was astounded. Poor Ameesh must have been tough for college's most popular singer to prove his identity.

"Ohh I'm sorry. I was just occupied."

"It's ok. So tell me how come you call??" I said enacting as if I was too naive to know anything.

"Hmm. So I suppose, Pulkit did not get to tell you anything about me."

"Pulkit????" I said as if I had heard this name for the first time.

"Ok." He took a deep breath and then spoke, "Aryan, buddy I want your help. Actually there were some errors in my mark sheet so I had sent it back to the University for making corrections. But they are behaving really evasively. "

"Hmmm, ok. So, I'm supposed to do what??"

"I have heard that an uncle of yours works there at a high post. So things can become easier if you talk to him on my behalf."

"Ohhh. So that is the situation."

"Aryan, I suppose you'll help me, being a friend" He said. 'Friend', now was not that a too fake word from his mouth?

"Of course, but see Ameesh, I can't talk to my uncle directly. But I can try asking dad to do that."

"Ok. But please do it yar, it is really important for me. And if you can help..." He mumbled for a minute longer and then we hung up the phone. In my mind, his words resonated again and again 'if you can help', yeah, that is what you heard me say Mr. Ameesh a year ago. Remember the way you treated me then.

How amazing it is, when with the passage of time, situations and circumstances remain same, but people swap positions. Once, I was pleading in front of a guy for an opportunity, but he shoved me away. After a lapse of 365 days, time was taking its toll. He was right there doing the same. And I was clear about the way, he deserves to get treated.

At a moment, I wished I would go and talk to dad about helping him. But my ego, the rage in my mind stopped me from doing that.

For now, I had managed to bring my 3rd and 4th semester's course to closing moments. And Sirat's exams were about to get finished too. Only one of them was left, so she was having a sigh of relief. She had declared it herself "in your services, highness. Just order me. How can this girl preclude herself from the offence of not helping the divine?" It all went over my head. God, she was so filmy.

"That is sooo cheesy. But I can make out from this that your exam went off well."

"Certainly. Finally, I'm out of the cage. "

"Not yet. There is one more to go." I brought her back to the reality.

"Yeah, but that's after 7 long days. I'll worry about it when 2-3 days will be left."

"That is what they call 'true engineering'. So tell me, are you ready with the questions."

"Yes, so here we go without any jokes."

"Exactly!"

"And sir, you won't make me laugh."

"Sirat, do I sound like a clown??"

"Tough question! Ok so sorry. But at least for the next 10 questions, nobody plays the kid, right?"

"That would be hard for you, mam. Now shall we, please??" I asked, pleading her.

"Ok so question 1......"

I answered 8 out of the 1st 10 questions correctly. Not only, she appreciated when I gave the right answer, it helped me to hike my confidence level too.

We kept doing this intriguing exercise for the next hour. We discussed the questions, or precisely she told me the things that I could not answer. Honestly, she did it so sincerely, that I did not feel shy or embarrassed to learn from a junior. Instead, I was contented to learn more. It was quite apparent that she too had worked on it.

"Thanks a lot for helping me." I told as we completed with the interrogation.

"You need not say this. Don't worry. I'm not doing it for you. " she said.

"Then who are you doing it for?? TCS! So that they get a pearl like me..!" I smirked at her.

"How modest. Well, I'm doing it for myself."

"Like what??"

"Like for that treat that you will owe me."

"Treat?? Which treat??" I said and both laughed.

Two days later, Ameesh called me again. "Hello." I picked up the phone.

"Hello. Aryan, how are you??"

"I'm pretty fine. You tell me??"

"I'm screwed up buddy." Finally the scoundrel admitted the truth. He added, "I'd told you about it two days ago."

"Yeah that's a real sort of mess." I tried to sympathize with my 'dear friend'.

"Hmmm. Did you talk to your dad about it??"

I was thinking hard to knit a story. "Yes. I did"

"Oh good, so he must have talked to your uncle. What did he say??" I kept quiet. At least give me a second, dude.

"Unfortunately no, actually dad tried but his family told that he had gone to Hyderabad for an educational conference."

"Ohh shit." He sounded disappointed. "Buddy, will you ask your dad to talk to him once more? Just once, please."

"I'll do that and let you know what happens."

"Ok, please try it soon. I fear I would be allowed to qualify for TCS if I don't get it shortly."

"Hmm. I understand. Don't worry, I'll see to it."

"I'll call you soon yaar. Please don't let my hopes down"

"Yes. I'll call you just as I get to know something. I have some urgent work. Bye."

"Ok bye-bye." I hung the phone and went back to pour my attention on what was actually important to me- my preparations.

The first job interview is one of things in life one can rarely forget. As I looked up in the mirror after dressing up in formal white shirt and black trousers, mixed feelings sprinted in me. It was going to be DIFFERENT today. After all, it was the days when my fate could be decided even if it was for a couple of upcoming years. I had been making careful preparations for it, and No matter what, I had to make them count. Though my family was equally excited and a bit nervous as I was, I was given a confidence boost before I left home for the placement drill.

The level 1 begin at 10 a.m. sharp and was a test confined to aptitude questions. Even though, it was not really tough, but I found most of my classmates, even those who were far better scorers that I was, exaggeratingly cribbing and panicking. I wondered whether that was supposed to be the code of conduct for the candidates. The results were out as the clock tick 2 O'clock. And I was in!

So what stood firm in front of me were the interviews, the real job! From day 1, I had been exposed to the fact that I don't look studious; I had worn antiglares to look somewhat intelligent.

Level 2~ The technical Interview Round

It had to be harder. And it demanded a lot more than just technical facts and concepts scrumming in your head. It needed confidence, and placidity. Even if I knew 100 things, and I was not able to convey even one of them, it would mean assured failure. Though I was playing cool from the morning, nervousness was building up. Thankfully, I was called for the interview before it overtook me completely.

In the interview room, everything depends on the way you answer the first question put up. For me, it was a soar. After one or two questions, the interviewer then asked me something Sirat had put upon me in the mock-interviews. And though I was not sure when I gave its answer to her, but today I was hell as confident about it. As the interview proceeded, I succeeded in making a good impression. Their expressions made it evident showed. They liked pedantic stuff I guess.

Just as I walked out of the room, I texted Sirat & told it to her, and that my interview went nice.

"Your resume speaks that you are a sheer believer of optimism, how??" the petite lady sitting in front of me, asked. To make it clear, she was the 'H.R.' executive of the recruitment team of the awaited 'TCS'.

And if you are confused, guessing my existence in front of her, I would remove all your doubts that I had reached the final level of getting selected- the H.R. interview. And this prestigious moment of sitting in front of her had come in my luck after succeeding in 1st two levels and slogging for past 15 hours.

I nodded in order to acknowledge her question when she spoke. The 1st thing that came to my mind was 'MUSIC'. I told her briefly about how I was attempting to make a music band from 2 and half years, subsequent failures did not stop me and I was not willing to give up yet.

“That’s quite impressive.” She said. Definitely, I was about to reach cloud nine, on hearing that. But she brought me back the next second by adding “But many people can take it as a form of stubbornness.”

“It is a matter of perception. But yes, I do feel that good end results can shut mouth better than good arguments. Mam, I suppose you’ll agree to this.” I did not mind using sugarcoating techniques, if they earn me a job, which pays 30,000 per month. But then who would?

“Undoubtedly I do. So, I’m done with the questions. We’ll let you know the rest very shortly.”

“Sure. Thanks mam.” She smiled.

After my interview, I was confident. It had gone well for me and I stood a good chance, at least I assumed it to be.

12 February 2011, 6:10 p.m.

I was wandering with my brother Ishu in our farms, when I checked my mailbox. There was a new mail in the inbox, the most valued & auspicious one of my career. It was from ‘TCS’

I had got selected. My hard work had been rewarded by god. Overjoyed, I was at the top of cloud nine. May be, I was not panicking like my classmates, but my happiness certainly had no limits. The next moment, I received a call from Pulkit and he told me that he too received the mail. Something I expected considering his abilities! I was curious to know who else had got placed amongst my classmates. And then Pulkit told me Manav, Rohit, Tanya have made it to TCS too. Long sigh!!!!

We went back home, to announce my achievement. Mom & dad were happy, proud, touched and everything they could be. The next moment, dad asked us to bring sweets. Indeed, it was time for celebrations for them. For now, I had secured a job, celebrated. I had eradicated the spot on my degree, thankfully. My command over

English had improved upon & still improving. Music, the best things always take the longest time!!

The fest was around, so getting a room allotted for practicing was not a tough job. The only tough part was making it useful. We started jamming together on 2nd march 2011. Our search for the bass guitarist had found solace in Anshul, Ajit's roommate. He was a polite & jovial guy, who met all our requirements. He was not that skilled, but his curiosity for playing guitar was immovable. That is all what we needed in him. He followed what we asked him to do. He took no time in buying a bass guitar. Though he was a novice with the instrument, but he was a fast learner which made my job easier. I had heard the Arpit playing the drums. It reflected that he had worked on it since, he played a way better than the last time.

With the amps and pedals, we had got solutions to many of the problems that we used to face. We had finally reached a stage, where we could start thinking about what songs we should play.

"Will you be able to sing Hindi songs?" I asked Ajit. I felt ridiculed at the same question I posed at him. He made a sore expression, like the one a drawing teacher makes, when he is asked to perform karaoke.

"I can't really say. I can, but it would be difficult to bona fide it as 'singing'."

I was wondering about what to say next, but then he added "I'm really comfortable at singing some English songs, yes." He looked really confident. I nodded.

"Ok, Thumb's up to that. It would be good if you can hymn anything in our native language, we need that." I said as I realized that he was waiting for my affirmation.

"Aryan is right; it is what actually makes the crowd rise to ecstasy." Arpit said, as we both looked at the Ajit with eyes full of expectations.

"I can do a 'Punjabi rap'. What do you have to say about that??" he said, after thinking for a while.

"That would be awesome..!!" I said. Yes, it would be thrilling.

Luckily, Arpit also gave a positive reaction. After all, I was craving, day & night, to formulate a band, which is different from others. And the only possible way was playing out-of-the-box music.

"So, what we want now is some nice popular English songs and rap. Audiences always enjoy what they have heard at least once." I told them.

Thought it took some debates out there, but we finally agreed to settle on 1 song of 'Linkin Park' and one rap by 'Honey Singh'. We started practicing the songs with enthusiasm. Things were going well, but somehow something seemed incomplete. When I shared this with my band mates, they got what I wanted to convey.

"Yes, I agree we desire another vocalist too." he said as matter-of-factly.

"No. We actually desire a female vocalist." I suggested.

"Female vocalist????" The three of them asked in unison. I had been expecting this.

"See, we want make our band unforgettable, do we??"

"yessss!!." They all nodded.

"We have got with us a rapper, who is promising enough. All's good with that. But at the end of the day, we cannot ignore the fact that conventional music is the forte of a music band. "

"Yeah that is understandable, but why specifically, a female singer only??" Ajit asked.

"Because nobody can haunt the audiences, as a girl can." Arpit spoke, and smiled to me. His line made me remember of Sirat. I wondered if he was a making a dig at me. Of course, that was my part of imagination, since nobody amongst them knew Sirat.

We had put a notice on the notice-board that announced our requirements of a female singer.

In the evening, I received a call from the Sameer. What would I tell him now, I asked my brain. Pick up the phone first, you idiot, it replied back.

“Hello.”

“Hello, sir.” After a bit of conversation, he asked me “sir, I’ve heard you are making the band.”

I had to tell him someday I knew. “You have heard it right. Sameer, look yar, I really wanted to involve you this time. But situations changed on my part.”

“Hmmm. I guess.”

“But please don’t take me wrong.”

“It is ok, sir. I can understand. And it is completely your choice.” His words made me feel relieved.

“Yeah so tell me, what are you doing on the fest? We do expect a solo performance.”

“Not solo. But yes, I’m making a music band this time.” I was shocked.

“A band, How come so soon??”

“I have found a fresher who plays drums really well, and a friend of mine who has agreed to give the bass. And I can play the rhythm, sir. ” he took pride in telling me that.

“oh really??.”

“Yeah, but we are trying hard, so let us see. Sir I wanted to ask you something as well.”

“go ahead.”

“I wanted to ask you if you’ll be playing the lead for our side.”

“You mean as the lead guitarist?”

“No no, we leave it up to your convenience. Be it through keyboard, or guitar.” He tried to convince me, for a couple of minutes.

"Sameer, you have always been nice to me. I do respect it. But I'm sorry; I can't join your band. I have already promised 3 guys, and I can't go back from my words, at the end moment." I denied his offer. There was one more reason behind it. I was not confident about them. I could not take the risk to believe in a band got constructed overnight.

But before we hung up, he said onething "but I was craving to perform with someone with experience, you, it would have done a world of good to us."

The next day, we began searching for a girl who could sing well, but that was not the only qualification we were looking for. Of course, we could not mention it in the notice, but I had borne in my mind that the 'girl-to-be-bestowed' must possess striking looks. After all, Looks did matter at least here.

Through auditions, we finally found a girl, who satisfied the necessities of our band. Her name was Payal. She sang quite ok, if not great, but she was the most prominent looking amongst all others who had shown up at the audition.

Taking into consideration her voice quality, we had selected 2 popular songs for Payal to sing. It took a lil time for her, but yes, she was giving her best not to let us down. The preparations for the fest have commenced in the college. So that meant no classes, full day practice, and lots and lots of disturbances by the people hovering around, aimlessly.

Who would not like to be surrounded by audiences, but certainly not in the practice sessions. Especially if the spectators scream every time your singer began to sing.

"All check??" I asked them, while the five of us were practicing for the performance in the practice room. They nodded.

"So here we all go for the ride." Ajit sang his part, and it was Payal's turn. She started singing her song well. One of the lines in her song had an equivocal meaning. When she sang it, the 'external factors' made a very loud roar. She looked really inconvenient, and got quite. Her reaction was quite expected by us.

"Don't worry. Ignore them." I said, trying to raise her spirits.

"Hmm. You can continue." Ajit said. After a couple of seconds, Payal regained some confidence, and started singing again. That had become a routine of practice for us.

Once she was singing her song, when the boys from outside passed some really terrible comments, which made her heart sank. That day, our comforting words & jokes could not manage to soothe her up. Amidst the practice, she left the practice room saying 'she needed a break'.

"Heya." I said as I saw her returning back to the practice room the next day.

"Hiii." She said looking bothered. But I did not ask her about it, thinking it might not be comfortable for her to talk about the last day.

"So, early today??" I asked her, breaking the awkward silence.

"Sir, I just came here to talk to you." She spoke after a while.

"Why not, tell me." I said.

I could see that she was finding hard to say, but then she said, "Sir, I don't think it would be possible for me to continue."

"So, what are you trying to say??"

"I mean the band & all, I want to withdraw myself."

I could not believe my ears, when she said that. I stood there, thinking of how to react to this ordeal. Should I malice, or yell, or plead to her.

I tried hard to convince her, but all in vain.

She finally said "I'm really sorry, sir. But I hope you'll understand." Yes, 'sorry' is the healer to all the tantrums you can throw at someone, at anyone.

"You need not to bother about that." I said, throwing hands away and looked towards the door. She walked out of it.

What was this now, god?? I had been scratching my heels over years, to formulate this band. And after coming to the verge of success, the loss of a vocalist can shatter my dream into pieces, again. And what was wrong with her. Of course, what happened a day before was no less. But what was my mistake in it.

Of course I could not tell this to this stupid dimwit. I did not want a sympathy vote even if it was the last chance. I told my band mates we needed to search for another vocalist in the nick of time.

"But we don't even have a complete week left in our hands."

"Do we have another option than trying??" of course, we could not waste more time in crying over the spilt milk.

……

In the core of my heart, I knew it would not be impossible to find another vocalist, since many girls had appeared on the auditions. We had started our quest again, and luckily we were getting results. We were hopeful that in a day or two, we would get an apt girl.

Meanwhile all this, we were getting a benefit unknowingly. News travel fast, making Payal realize that she was missing out on something people generally crave for. She could see that our loss of a vocalist was now transforming in to her own loss.

While I was practicing with my mates, she called me up. I came out of the room, And I picked up the phone.

"Hello."

"Hello, sir. Please don't disconnect the phone." She said hurriedly assuming that I was going to do so. If I would have to disconnect, why would I have bothered up picking it anyways. I did not speak, but stayed on the line, waiting for her to say that she had called up for.

"Sir, I wanted to talk to you about something." Now, this line had begun to frighten me. Usually, People tend to use it as an introducing weapon to all the tortures.

"What is it?" I said in a no-nonsense tone.

"Sir, I'm really very sorry about that absurd behaviour of mine. I realize that it should not have been done." She apologized.

"It is good for you to know that. Anything else you want to say, or... " ok, maybe, I was getting too rude, but that is what she was ought to get.

"Yes, sir. I wanted to ask if...." she was finding hard to say what she wanted to. But I was in no mood to mollify her nervousness. And then she gave me another jolt.

"Sir, may I re-join your band please??"

"Come again. What did you just say??"

"sir, I have realized in the past 1 and a half day, that I've thrown an axe at my own feet by saying 'no', and I do regret it but ...." she mumbled for some more minutes.

"Sir, can you please say something now??" She asked me

"I can't sit in the ivory tower and judge, whether you should be allowed to come back. We'll discuss about it and tell you." I hung up the phone, saying this.

"Payal called just now." I came back in the practice room and told them.

Three of them threw confused looks at me, only till Arpit gave voice to their thoughts.

"What did she say??"

"She wants to make a comeback in our band."

"Really?? She said all this by herself." Ajit asked me.

I nodded. He looked relieved. "So, we should bring her back. What did you tell her??"

"Wait a second, Ajit." Arpit told him and turned his eyes to me.

"What is your take, Arpit??" I asked him

Perplexed, he shrugged. Ajit raised his eyebrows.

Arpit said," I can't say, man. She walks out of the situation any time, and rings up to apologize for it, the next day. Is this a hoax??"

"Exactly. It would not be that easy for us."

"But do you think she is willing enough this time??"

"She does sound convincing. So, let us just consider it."

"But.... " he protested a lil.

"Look dear, I understand that what she did was completely wrong, but we need to think rationally, we practically have just 4 days left. Of course, it would be difficult for us to adjust with her now, but it'll be far easier than finding a new girl and guide her. Isn't it??"

"It is, for sure." And then no more interrogations were made by Arpit."

Payal called me half an hour later. "Sir, what have you guys decided and made your mind??"

"See, Payal it's not easy for us."

"So does that means...." disappointed, she stopped without completing her sentence.

"That means it involved a stretched discussion. You are invited back, only if"

"Only if??"

"You take it meaningfully."

"I would, sir. I promise, and things would not get repeated."

"There's one more thing."

"Yes sir??"

"Ya, reach the practice room tomorrow sharp at 9 a.m."

So finally things returned on the track. I wished crossed fingers till the final moment. The moment had come when we were asked to get our band's name registered for performance in the BATTLE OF BANDS.

"But we have not decided the name, as yet." Arpit said.

"Hardly matters buddy, we'll do it now." I said.

"Sir, what should be like?? Music??"

"Maybe, or may be related to us??" Arpit said.

"Boys of beat.", Said Ajit.

"Sorry, dear. But Yuck!!!" Anshul said as we laughed.

"Never mind. By the way, there's something common between the 4 of us." I said

"Let me say, the first letter of our name. They all begin with 'A'. Is it??" Anshul said, and raised his eyebrows for my conformation. He was quite observant I knew. And that was one of the key that made him learn the guitar so finely in such a short span. I nodded.

"Exactly. the 4 a's" Arpit said.

"How about 4 ace's. See each one of us is symbolized by an ace in the deck of cards, making it complete. " Ajit said and smirked.

"That sounds good too."

"Yes, but we are forgetting someone .But Payal??" Anshul said, they all looked perplexed.

"Hmmm. What about the 5th one, her name does not even have 'a' as an alphabet??" Ajit said.

"Gottcha, man. The 5th one. So let's call it '5th ace'." I thought I had solved our dilemma.

"That's unmistakable, man" Arpit said and smiled at me. The rest two hi-fived.

The list of the band's participating in the fest, included 1 more new name- MOKSHA. To my astonishment, MOKSHA was Sameer's band. He had succeeded in doing what actually took 3 years of my engineering. But I did not envy him. A bit of shock, but no jealousy I was sure. On the other hand, 'VISHESH' was not just participating, but also formed a chunk of the main organizer's team for music. Two more bands from other colleges were coming to perform, so I realized it was not going to be a cake walk for us.

The ultimate day, 30th/march/2011.

Finally, the day I was waiting for had arrived. The crucial day fetched many different feelings got aroused inside me, feelings that I had hardly seen in me, ever before. I had tossed over the bed last night.

The next day was special not just for me, but it was an awaited day for many others. Our senior batch's convocation was scheduled on the morning. Kunal and Tushar had come to college to collect their degrees and that black robe it evoked amazing excitement. Imagining that I would wear that robe next year, an automatic smile flashed on my face. The glint of pride in their eyes was worth 4 years of exertion.

I was with my band mates as I saw Kunal from a distance. His looks had changed a lot in one year. And he, though was always among the studs of college, looked better. He waved at me, I walked up to him.

"Congratulations, bro." I said as we shook hands.

"Thank you, dear. How were you doing?"

"I'm doing good. How's the job going? Are they really blood-sucking?"

"Uhmm, I don't want to scare you."He laughed mutely and then added, "But yes, I miss college and the fest more than anything. It was fun, no?"

"The fun is yet to begin." I said with a smirk at my face. Kunal gave me a what-is-it look."

"I have made a music band. And it's gonna be our first performance tonight." I said.

"Oh my, your own band! Wow, man. Now that's something." He said, a genuine happiness reflecting in his eyes. I asked him if he would be staying that night.

"I would have loved to, but I'm afraid I'll have to leave in an hour or so." I understood his dilemma. I waved him a good-bye. But, I still remember his words clearly when he said, "Good luck buddy, make sure it makes home in the minds of 'Vishesh'."

In the evening, when a few minutes were left in our performance, I could almost hear my heartbeat. Questions were popping up in my mind, making me uneasy every passing second. Apart from Ameesh and Rohit, Tushar had also joined them backstage. But, I applaud my senses that helped me.

Suddenly, I received Sirat's phone call. I could not hear her much because of the noise around, so I hung the phone telling her that. She texted me next minute. It said:

"Don't worry. You have done your job, god will now do his. Enjoy the moment you have longed for. Good luck"

I smiled & replied to her "Thanks is too small a word for you."

We were just about to get called on the stage. I was trying hard to compose myself, by telling myself that I was not performing on stage for the 1st time, so these feelings were not meant to block my way, at any cost. We decided to shuffle Payal's song after 1st two songs by the Ajit, So that, we could conclude with the Punjabi rap.

When we went on the stage, it was close to 7:30 pm. I realized I was finally collecting myself to some extent. Music was helping me to gain senses again. It took almost 5 minutes to do the sound check, during which I tried ignoring talking to Ameesh, Rohit, as much as I could. I went to the drummer to give the final commandment a minute before.

As our 20-minutes long performance started, dim blue lights filled the atmosphere. It made every visible thing beautiful by manifolds. The enchanting night, beautifully adorned college, those twinkling lights, and cheering faces, life at that moment was so magnificent. Believe me from the top, the audience looked better than all my anticipations.

The dim lights jazzed up as we proceeded further. They pepped us right from the beginning. Even though I was tensed like anything, it helped me play with all my concentration. I had to assure nothing goes wrong.

But with passing moments, things began to seem easy. I was finally on the stage that I have craved about from an era. I was finally performing to the people I have been a part from ages. I could see people where enjoying our performance. Payal's entry made the crowd roar at the top of their voice. She sang well & fulfilled the responsibility given to her. The raps thrilled the audiences. Performing to that audience, I was happy that my efforts yielded & brought me up.

The performance went well, by heaven's grace. I stepped down from the stage, but I was at the zenith of happiness, a place from where I did not want to return, at least not for a long time. I had fulfilled my wish, my dream. A feeling of content had taken birth in me. I was satisfied, I had finally done it. I went to Pulkit.

"Finalllly... congrats, man." He hugged me.

"Thanks." I was falling short of words.

"Unbelievable!! You guys rocked, it's fun watching your best friend on stage, but you made me feel envious." Pulkit winked.

"Yeahhii. That was the aim of my life." I said and we laughed. Some classmates joined us. I hardly remember the last time, any one of them ever come to me, with a wide smile. Today, they were beaming, shaking hands with me.

"That was a great performance, Aryan."

"Yup, never seen something so different in our college."

"Keep it up, man, and Ajit was a real hunk!!" just the rapper?? Oh, though I gave an unusual hint but I frankly did not bother. I could not spoil my day.

As our performance ended, Vishesh stepped up on the stage. I was in a really good mood, and how illogical it may sound, watching their performance would have done a mood-spoiling job for me. So, I gave Pulkit some excuse, and departed from there. I came towards the cafeteria which was depopulated. But I preferred sitting in abundance over cheering up for Vishesh.

As I sat there still, my mind replayed the last few moments over and over again. Our performance, those applauses, those praises had made way. The criticism, the disapproval had faded away. As time passed, the cafe got crowded. I saw some of my acquaintances, they poured blessings, complements. They were chameleons, whose opinion mattered to me the least. But I wanted to meet someone, the girl who did not change her mind, who supported me when no one else did. I called Sirat to meet me in the cafeteria.

In less than a minute, she arrived. And I saw her from a distance. Just as she reached to her, her eyes widened, and she said, "Ohh goodness!! What a thrilling performance. The rapper in your band has such an electrifying stamina, that he has almost exhorted us. " that was all she said.

"Hmm. Yeah." What else was I expected to say to her. I was taken aback by what I just heard, what shocked me more was it was Sirat who had said it.

'What about me?' I wanted to ask her, but I did not.

"Really, his power packed voice was the real icing in your performance." I smiled in a fake manner. Unfortunately, to maintain it was turning out to be tough. I wanted to go away from her.

She talked about every other thing, the fest, the quizzes, her comparing, our performance. But I had lost interest in talking to her. However, I did not want to piss her off, so I kept answering whatever she asked.

I came back, making an excuse that I had to catch up with my classmates. She went off to handle the stage after a while. While watching her announcing on the stage, I wondered how she couldn't find that something was wrong. That something she had done pinched me. But I was sure about 1 thing if it were someone else, who had said something like that, I would not have bothered that much.

Not this way, I wish

I was expecting that the night after the fest would be the most peaceful one. However, the expected never happens, at least not in my world. I went through all the things that happened to me in the fateful day. I gained a million things, and lost the countless. I had fulfilled my desire, my passion. I had an upper hand over those who never thought I'll end up successfully. I had gained content.

But there was a hint of restlessness in a corner of my mind. I could not stop my mind from indulging into the thoughts about Sirat, thoughts that sprung me away from her. How her eyes widened while she was praising Ajit, the moment I met her after my performance. Was she the same girl who had always known my weak spots?? I wondered if she was the same girl who saw me striving for my performance day & night.

I wondered how people could give all the credit to one person when everybody has donkey-worked on it. Maybe that was what made Tushar bother. Maybe these feelings were responsible for making him aggravated him against Kunal. I could now understand why "Vishesh" got split in the 2nd year fest.

On The final eve of prize distribution, we were all present to see the results. As per my expectations and their 3-year long performing experience, 'Vishesh' got the first prize. We stood 2nd, but I was contented that we performed and outraced 3 other bands.

The internal exams after the fest were a catastrophe. For the 1st time, I was least bothered about giving them. I skipped 2 out of 4 exams. And, yes all this seemed usual to us, considering we had reached the final year. I wonder how could I be so mad about the same thing, 3 years ago.

The time to part was approaching, everybody was aware of this. The classrooms started remaining vacated. And we had begun to sit in groups and chit-chat. Something we rarely thought of doing after 1st year, when everyone was everyone's friend. The month of April was at its closing stages.

Sirat called to meet me one day. She insisted me to give her the treat that I owed her. So, I agreed readily since I had promised her and after all the help that she had given me, she completely deserved it. This was our first proper meeting after fest. We met in the cafeteria, after the college got over. After the treat, we came out to the corridor which was the usual venue for holding all our ad-hoc meetings.

"So tell me something how's college going?? I mean final year, that too about to end??" She asked

"Yeah, seems tough to leave the place. I spend most of the time with my classmates now, no more than 2 classes in a day. I'll miss the place, I suppose."

"Just the place?? Not the people here??" she asked.

"Not really, but maybe someone is an exception."

"Who?? Who??" she asked, her eyes lit up.

"My best friend, Pulkit."

"Bet he can't be the only one." She said as I told her a few more names, many of them were names that I hated, names that irked me. I finished.

"Ohh." She looked disappointed, as I finished.

"Something wrong with that??"

She moved her neck, saying no. But I could see something was bothering her.

"You're concealing something. Tell me is there something that's making you worried??."

"Yeah, I guess." she thought for a couple of minutes and then spoke.

"I think our bond is that strong now, that we can speak our hearts out to each other." I nodded.

She took a long sigh. "Sir, remember the first time I met you."

I did remember it well, and, with years passing by us had brought a sea change between us. That confident girl I saw around 3 years ago wearing blue gloss had become one of my dearest friends.

"Well, the only day you looked innocent to me, madam. 'I'm-very-shy' types?? Huh??" I said and laughed. She did too, but only a little. I wondered why she was talking about this. She had always been the one to brush away this topic.

"Yeah, you remember that well, but I was seriously very shy in at the moment."

"Ohoho. How easy is to believe that when I know you this well?" I teased and then added as an afterthought, "things have changed a lot." I said.

"But something did not." she kept mum and then spoke again. "My feelings did not. I like you even before I existed for you. From the moment I saw you at my fresher's eve, I have thought about you. And maybe you know or not, I have never stopped doing it from the past 2 and half years. I just could not."

That was a kick in the teeth. I did not know what to say. I wished that I was being fooled. Don't know for how long, I stared at her hoping if she would laugh out the next moment and say all that she said was a prank or dare or anything but not the truth. She did nothing of that sort.

"Why did not you tell me this, earlier??"

"But you knew this, sir. I mean it was easy to find out."

"It wasn't, Sirat." I told her. Even if I had the slightest clue about it, I was in no state to tell that to Sirat, at least not then, when she was standing in front of me, pouring her heart out. In those moments, a couple of occasion when I heard her lines as weird ran in front of my eyes. Some things which Sirat said as a joke had an undercurrent meaning. I wish I was good enough to understand her subtle ways.

"Hmmm.Ok, Let's say, it was not. But now I have told you everything, so??" she said and turned into a stone the next second.

"So what?? What are you expecting now??" I bulldozed her to speak up. For the first time, making her speak was getting tough.

"What do you expect from the person you like?? You can understand that well." She looked at me hopefully.

"I do. So anything else you want to say."

"I don't want you to go."

"Who are you to say that? If you remember, we were just friends." I took a breath, moved my eyes away from hers and then continued speaking.

"I've never known of your intentions. If I had known, then I would not be standing here. I would have never become friends with you." I looked back at her, even her expecting eyes could not stop me from shunning her off. But I was bound to look away. I guess one needs to move the gaze, before breaking someone up. It just gives you the necessary strength you require to do it.

"Sirat, I've just 3 months left to leave the place, so I'm not in a stage to promise you anything. Just because I talk to you, consider you a friend, gives you no right to portray things. There's hardly any future can see with you, not even in your wildest dreams. Getting??"

I managed to look at her. She was already looking at me, our eyes met. She was about to cry, anyone could easily guess. She wanted to say something, but she did not. Why are you doing all this, I felt like she wanted to ask me. But it was not my mistake; I always took her as a friend, a very close friend but nothing more than that.

She looked away, just the moment I was going to break the eye-contact.

"What was all that, when you called me your closest friend?? We have been sharing almost every matter, over so long." She stood just 3 inches away from my face, as she said that.

"Exactly I'm fond of you as a 'friend'; it is you who picked me wrong."

"I did. It was a big deal. And trust me sir, you don't even know what you mean to me."

"I don't even want to know." I almost screamed it to her and cursed myself the next moment on watching her tremble like that.

"I think I'll walk back." she said, fighting a lump in her throat. I did not stop her and we started walking in the direction of her hostel. There were very few people in the lane, since it was quite late, so I was comfortable performing the custom of seeing her off to the limit. But there was a huge difference today. Titters on her face had got replaced by sobs. The guy responsible for it was walking along her.

While walking back, I saw some of my acquaintances sitting in the lane from a distance.

"Oh shit, how could Tarun be here??" Sirat who had been walking, looking towards the floor, moved her eyes up & saw them. I did not want to get in to an embarrassing situation.

She understood and her voice broke a little, as she said "I can walk back alone. I don't ..." she kept mum. After a short while, she said, "You can go."

I realized I could not afford to get spotted with a girl, who is a minute short of breaking in to tears. "I'm already going for ever." Her heart sank. Our eyes met again. I was struggling to look into them. I said "bye". She did not answer & walked away from me, in the direction of her hostel. After a second she left, I looked around to find that it was exactly the same lane I met her for the 1st time. Things are no longer the same as they were that day. Not even a bit.

Guilt flushed inside me while I made my way back to home. Thoughts of Sirat clouded in my mind, thoughts about the first time I saw her, thoughts about the time that made her my closest friend, and thoughts about the last few minutes when I shattered her without giving a second thought. My heart cramps when I imagined her being pierced. The girl, who just needed half a sentence from me to know that I was upset, was reduced to tears. And to the worst, it was me who was responsible for bringing them on her.

May be, if I would have given a second thought, I would not have treated her the way I did. She did not deserve those tears. May be if I would have recalled how she stood by me in ups & downs, how she took chances just to help me in her finals, how she was willing to be on my side every time, how it made a difference to me when she praised someone else, I would not have shoved her away from me. Infinitely away.

I had no other option than bearing the guilt brought by my own actions. I shivered as I imagined her condition when I had left her alone. How could I do that? How could anyone on earth do that?? May be, I should have said a 'yes to her'. Maybe I should but after a couple of months, or a year when I'll have to go?? She would have been on the top of the world. But it was just going to be momentary happiness, something that is assured to end. And, leaving her after coming even closer would leave a wound much greater than what I gave her that day. I had to win over the soft corner of my heart that I had given to her thoughts. I had to think practically which was good not only for me, but for her too. However if I had one wish granted from god, I would take no time to decide what I want from him. My only wish is to erase that one day from my life. The moment of ill-luck that snatched an angel from me.

…………

"Ohh, but we can't blame all of it on her." Pulkit said, as he came to know about Sirat.

I threw him a look, which strange enough to make him understand that he should not weigh up our faults, sitting in the ivory tower.

"Now what?" He asks, as he tries to restart the conversation.

I shrugged, and took a long sigh.

"Ok, let's face the truth man. Look Aryan, this is between two of us, so tell me the truth. Do you like her?"

Taken aback, I made the sorest kind of expression I can, "Of course not, and of all the people on this planet, you are asking me this question? Had it been the case, I would have told you from ever, man."

"I know, but now that you're behaving this silent, anybody could suspect that."

"Suspect what?"

"Those feelings for her have aroused in you. I think so…"

"You are free to think whatever pleases you." I said cutting him, amid of his sentence, irked by his last statement.

"Ok, calm down. Did you guys talk after that?" Pulkit said, making an expression one cannot shun easily. I really did not have to be ruthless with every person alive. I tried to calm myself down, as the last I wanted to happen now was watching him walk out.

"She did not call. And so did I." I said and then added as an afterthought, "To make some distance." I guess, I needed to tell the reason to myself more than to Pulkit.

"After she has told you all this, you hate her, do you?"

"I don't know." I said, without paying any second thoughts. I could not hate her. In the frame of my manipulative mind, I still felt Sirat was a kid, who was just infatuated. A corner of my heart asked if infatuations survive for as long as 3 years.

"Hmmm. So, you don't love her, neither do you hate her, man? At least make it clear what you want."

"I don't know, I mean I wish we could remain friends like we used to be."

"Oh c'mon, stop acting like a girl wanting to cling to this 'friends forever' notion. Either let her go or."

"Or screw her? Huh?"

"That's not how I meant it, Aryan. And you know that well." I did, but I was in a mess not to think wise at that point of time. It was funny that I was feeling creepy as if I was the one who fell for Sirat, and not her.

"I'm sorry."

"It's ok. You just need to admit the fact that these things could happen to anyone."

"Yeah, but why her? Pulkit, I know it was not her fault. But how am I supposed to react when one of my best friends admits that she had fell for me years back, I'm the last one to know about it. I'm not fortunate enough keep her by side, just because I don't want to leave her shattered after a year or so. She turns out to be totally frail, breaking herself down and making me feel guilty. And, what I'm I left to do in the end? Watch her walk away?" I said and then added, "Just because I can't get on to this long distance kind of crap. Nobody does. This relationship would have got her nowhere we both know. How do I shut my eyes to that?" Hearing my words, Pulkit shrugged. Though I expected him to speak, but he did not say a word.

………

Some days later, I met Ajit in the college. He waved at me. It took me a bit more than the usual to recognize whether his new hairdo was the result of a pitfall made by the stylist or Mr. rapper's own idea.

"Here we go, the new hairstyle. Ahem ahem." I said, making a dig at him.

"Nice, isn't it?? It took me almost half-an-hour to explain this to the guy." He said, bragging his new look. In fact, his accent appeared quite transformed. Now where was that coming from?? Hollywood, I guess.

Nice???? Tough question!! But I hided my smile and nodded at him. I realized he was at cloud nine that day.

"Ohh, so tell me how many proposals have you received??" I asked him.

"Actually, I have stopped counting now."

"Really????"

"Yeah. Wonder if girls have something else to do here than just day-dreaming." He continued to blow his own trumpet. And his expressions while saying that were making me laugh. But I tried to control & composed an expression to appear really sympathetic towards the new post-fest 'rockstar'.

"Anyways, I'll catch you later sir, I need to go. Bbbyyee. "

"Sure. Bye." he left. Thank god, now I could at least laugh.

Our last semester at college was much alike the very 1st one in the sense that now most of the groups of our entire class has fused into each other, forgetting every rift. I guess it was because of the grim realization that the time of our parting was not far. I was fooling around with my classmates in the cafeteria when I saw Sirat.

The last I met her was 9 days ago. It was the same day that I broke her heart. That was the 1st time I saw her after that. Though, she could not see me, but from my point of view she was fairly visible. Or maybe she was trying to ignore looking around so that she could not find her culprit. Sirat had come over with her classmates, but rarely in those 10 minutes, I saw her talking to anyone of them. After a couple of more minutes, her gaze fell upon me. I was already looking at her. To say the least, she looked the same way as I had left her 9 days ago.

I was expecting my presence to get acknowledged but she lowered eyes without reacting much. I was guilt-ridden on watching her doing that. With every passing minute, I had a sudden urge to walk upto her. An inexplicable urge to explain myself to her. An urge to ask her why was she being such a kid, and where the hell she had lost that contagious smile. And to tell her that, to hell, it still mattered to me. There are more things important in life; I wished I could make her understand. But I could not afford to create more issues for her.

Fortunately, a few moments later Sirat looked at me again. This time, her expression little softened. Battling against my ruthless mind, I picked up my cell-phone and gave up my ego, and texted her:

"I hope I don't look that scary, but tell me do I?"

I saw Sirat checking her phone the next moment, but she did not care to answer me back. I wondered what was so captivating on the floor of the cafeteria as her eyes riveted to it. I mean, she really did not have to think like I had put up a million dollar question. She cared to reply me back but after 5 long minutes.

"No."

Unfortunately, those five minutes were enough to make my mood go upside down, to boil me up. A million things were running in my mind to write back to her but I ended up writing just 6 words:

"Can't you forget all that happened?"

“That would be like turning my face from harsh reality. Please, don’t expect anything of that sort from me, Sir.”

“Then accept the reality. Look at yourself, Sirat. You’re ruining it for yourself.”

“I’m not. Sir, can you please stop making this more difficult?”

“Why are you punishing yourself??”

“I’m not punishing myself. And even if I’m, I deserve this, Don’t I?”

“Sirat, I have no clue what you are up to. For my sake, move on.”

“I’m left too behind to do that. You don’t worry, I can handle my life.”

Honestly, reading those words, my world blacked out for a second.

“Do as you wish.” I finally wrote back. My eyes met her face before I came out of the cafeteria.

Even the moments of our fresher’s party were fidget fresh in my mind, when I heard the news that our farewell party had been decided in ‘Hotel Modesty’ on 7th may 2011,as it was decided by our juniors.. The last party of my engineering stood there right next to me. How fast time flies in front of one’s eyes. I could not stop the time. No one could. But I wanted to make it memorable for myself.

One evening when I was busy making choices about my apparel, Nikhil called me up. He was a year junior to me. But I had known him for years, since we shared the same school with each other.

He said “A guy called Manav is disturbing the preparations we have made for the ‘farewell’.”

“How come?? What does he want??” I asked him.

“Actually, he has collected 7-8 other people from the final year. And just 3 days before the party, they are demanding for a change in the venue to Hotel C.R.. We would have tried but we have already made some advance payments to the "Hotel Modesty". So it has ended up in a huge fuss.”

"Hmm, but hotel modesty was chosen because it was a way better than C.R."

"Uhm, and almost all of your classmates had given their consent to that, on Friday. But now they are turning their back now." Nikhil said, as a matter-of-factly.

"Ohh I see. Have you guys tried to sort it out one-to-one with him??"

"We have tried more than once, but he's being too adamant. I thought to talk to some senior who could help us. So, you were the first name in my mind."

"I can see you have a right point, so I would not doing that, for sure. And don't worry; nobody wants their farewell party to get spoilt, so hopefully they might not mind bending a bit."

I hung up the phone & thought what was meant to be done. Manav was never a friend of mine, but Tanya's love for him along with his ways in the past was enough to make him adore the list of 'my silent rivals'. So, calling him up would mean a squirm on my ego. But I could not let him do everything the way likes, so I found his contact number, and called him up. After a bit of normal 'hi-how were you' chat, I asked him for what I called him.

"Why do you want the farewell to be held at C.R. instead of Hotel Modesty??" yes, I admit hating every inch of him but while asking this question, I took special care of my tone. I kept it polite.

In the last few days, I did not want to get remarked as rude by any one. I wanted to make the ending of my engineering 'pleasant' for others. For me, I was always nasty to many of them. Of course, that was only my preference over being pretentious.

"Ohh, but it's just not me now. I have talked with many of our friends who want the venue to be altered. You have a problem with that??" towards the end of his statement, his tone had become quite contradictory to mine.

"Not me, but those who have organized the party do have."

"You mean our juniors." Of course, who else would I mean by that, the house-keeping department of 'hotel Modesty'??

"Yeah. Actually, they have already paid some share of the payment ...." I was speaking when I heard the tone of my phone. The last call cost message flashed, indicating the phone call got disconnected.

Ahh, these network errors have such a perfect timings, I thought to myself. And I dialed his number again. This time, he disconnected the phone without even picking it up. I understood that it was not the network responsible for the last call's abrupt cut off. Rather, Manav was sick enough to be blamed for running off. Bloody coward.

Half an hour later, I texted a message to him:

We'll do the party where it has been decided. Stop it if you can.

He replied back:

"Listen you f*#%! # m&^#@ , it would be better if you s#uc#$%s^% stay out. Bl#$%%. . Swear......... "

After a minute, I received another one. He was such a pimp. I wanted to come back with the f*#!in bastard in his own language, but I controlled my anger. I decide not to rebut, not to abuse him back. It was not the best time to answer, I kept my patience. I knew I would get a better time to teach him a lesson. Eager I was, but I waited for the right occasion to come.

Next day in the college, Computers-3rd year and 4th year students assembled in the cafeteria to resolve the matter. We came to know that Manav had managed to plot & persuade a majority of hostellers to get on his side, in just one night. I had become insensitive to this, after spending years in a class full of unreliable hostellers.

In the morning, Nikhil and his friends had requested to me to stand by them. I told them that I would not step back from my words, and I'll try to convince my classmates thoroughly.

When I saw Manav, my insides got blistered with fury. Tanya like always was being the backbone of her sweetheart. But I tried to divert my attention by talking to Pulkit & the juniors. After sometime, the moment came when I had to confront him, talk to him face to face. I kept my point against him. In his air, he hardly paid any heed to my words. He interrupted in between, but I stopped him bluntly, asking him to wait till I completed.

When he was asked to speak, he preferred yelling. What else is expected from people who can't quote significant explanations for their useless demands?

It would not be wrong, if he was titled as the most annoying creature. Just as I turned back to leave the place, he caught hold of my right wrist all of a sudden and gave me a jerk. He must have not expected how much he would have to pay for that action of his. Before a moment to pass, I pulled out my left hand, and placed a tight slap on his right cheek. I made sure that I should make that one as hard as possible. Quite unexpectedly, he fell off to the direction of my hand.

Seeing some teachers around, a sudden hustle-bustle got uproar in the cafeteria. I'm sure if anyone of them had caught hold of me, it would have resulted in guaranteed pack-up from the college that day. Pulkit & Nikhil standing behind me pulled me back. Away from the situation. While I was being pulled back, I glanced at her. Sirat stood at a distance, looking at me in fret. Even in a crowd of a hundred, I could recognize her. But before I managed to make out something else, she got off my sight.

The most enjoyable slap I could deliver not only insulted Manav, but also made the junior girls go mad with worry. For a moment, they thought of backing out from the farewell party. Though, it involved giving them stretched assurance, but somehow the matter got suppressed.

After 2-and a half hour, I decided to talk to some of my brainy classmates to negotiate a solution. I talked to everyone, and tried hard to convince them courteously.

I even told them that hardly anyone from 3rd year was willing to attend the party at 'Hotel C.R.'. I told them it would bring them a loss of thousands. And that the farewell without juniors would mean just a simple get-together. But they did not see eye to eye with me. Like always.

People who I called 'friends' for the last four years, people who I never said 'no' to, people who I helped in every situation I could, did not agree to me. They were too inflexible to compromise, to adjust. They chose 'Hotel C.R.' as the venue for the 'farewell' party.

That eve, I texted Sirat. "Were you present in the cafeteria??"

She replied. "Yeah, it was me. I saw you from a distance."

"Oh. So will you be attending the farewell??" I wrote the question that was bothering me & send it to her.

"No. I too was on your side." In hearts of my hearts, her answer contented me. It meant a lot.

"Ok." She did not reply after that.

The next day, Pulkit asked me to pay the money for farewell party.

"Have you gone mad??" I asked him.

"Since the day I found you in life. But what is it now??"

"Pulkit, how can I go for this 'farewell'?? I do suppose I have some self-respect existing inside me."

"Look Aryan, I know you are taking sides but it is our farewell party!! Do you even realize we have been waiting for this? Even you were so keen, so now how do you expect us to miss this??"

"Excuse me, I'm not going & I'm not asking you to stay. You are making me angry now."

He kept mum, when I added. "Feel free to do what your heart says."

"Thanks a lot for your permission, sir." Disgust was written all over Pulkit's face.

"Anything else??" I said, as he walked out.

Though, it took one complete day for my thick-head to realize that I was being extra rude to Pulkit, that too, due to no fault of his. But when this fact finally registered my mind, I wasted no more time to call him up. After 2 minutes of uncomfortable one-sided conversation, I made up my mind and said:

"I'm sorry, man. I should not have spilled beans on you yesterday. I'm really very guilty."

"Oh shut up you idiot, and for god's sake stop sounding like you are apologizing to your girlfriend." He said and laughed, thinking of my stupidity.

"So, is the suit ready??" I asked.

"Which suit??"

"The one you gave for stitching for the farewell party."

"Ohh that one. I've changed my mind."

"Why?? That suit was nice."

"No, about the farewell."

"Are you kidding me?? But why????" I felt guilty.

"I guess, they'll be able to do without me. But how have I enjoyed without my only friend's company."

We did what I had never thought of. We missed our own farewell. Pulkit missed his farewell for me. He was one crazy guy I could rarely find any competition for. Most of the past few years, I had hated him for giving me a bit say in the things that primarily belonged to me, but now that I see back, I find myself lucky to have this jerk in my life.

I was satisfied to do what my conscience told me. For me, my 'ego' was prior to the festivity. Most of the juniors too stayed at their words by not attending the farewell, which had now got restricted into a get-together.

My heart had given it up from my classmates. A mere thought of their faces even began to annoy me. Some of them even apologized to me after the party. But it hardly made a difference to me. The way they snubbed me, when I asked them for support, had left an imprint on my mind.

Exams started within no time. The 4-subject course went like a walk in the park, short & easy. 4 days after the last exam, one of my classmates called me and asked to come to the college. It was time for hostellers to depart. I refused to go back to them, who did not even deserve a good-bye in my sight.

The college ended.

Getting paid back..!

Back at home, the first 4-5 days, it felt quite similar to the way it was around 4 years ago, when after I had wrapped up with my AIEEE exam, that same relaxation, the monotonous idleness and the long wait. Then I was waiting for my college life to begin & now I was waiting for my career to get a start. The days were the longest I had ever seen. And that was when time hardly seemed to move. Boredom definitely has the potential to drive one crazy. Silently perhaps.

Life had come to standstill but lucky enough, I had received my offer letter from TCS before I thought I would be overcome by idleness. It was turn for the joining letter, which accounted for my primary concern.

Usually, the calling used to start from the month of October – November. So I was pleased that I could spend some time at home. I had heard enough to believe that the next years were going to be occupying, so it was time to take a summer break. Plus, I wanted to enjoy the final 'leisure' vacation, taking as much rest as I could, where rest means sleeping like a horse.

Courtesy to mom's comments that I received every morning, I realized it was not the moon yet. I started utilizing time in brushing up my general knowledge and communication skills by reading newspaper and hanging onto various news channels. The call centres in the nearby metro-cities emerged as an attraction. As they were good enough to provide a seasonal employment, so, many of my associates, as I heard, were pulled towards them. Deep analysis over the pro's and con's of the call centre thing made me conclude that I was in no mood to leave my town so ardently for it.

Also, the new session was about to start, so many colleges in the vicinity had offered vacancies for the post of assistant professors. Even if it was getting difficult to pass time at home, none amongst them amused me, at all. But I gave a try in my own college. The reason of course was its close location to my home.

It seemed funny that the same college that I was running away from, when I was 17, now pulled me back. What was even funnier that now I was keen to become a part of it, even for just a few months more. But fatefully, only those who did not get placed within the campus were eligible. Of course, they needed the job more.

Amidst of all this, there was one thing that I never left behind, music. I could survive without food for days, but music was my oxygen, my rehab, and not a mere stand-by. When I wanted to talk to someone and my contacts seemed in dearth, I picked up my guitar. It never gave me a 'no'. When I was bored & restless, I choose playing keyboard. When I missed college and wanted to go back, I played harmonica even more and everything would get fine in minutes. Music was the icing on my plain cake. It soothed me in every moment of discomfort.

Once in a while, Ajit gave me a call.

"Hiii."

"Oh hii." that was the first time I had received his call after the fest, so it was a bit surprising. "How come you call today??"

"Sir actually, I'm formulating a new music band."

"New music band??"

"Yeah, you must be aware that after Arpit & your absence, our band has got almost split into chunks. But luckily for us, you'll stay in the same place for??"

"For around 2-3 months, probably."

"Yeah, and similarly Ameesh & Rohit's absence had made a loss to 'Vishesh' which now means just Jatin & their drummer." He said, as I was dazed by 'Vishesh' being mentioned.

"So??"I asked

"So, I have discussed with them and we have planned collaboration, so that we can play together as one. They'll be playing guitar & drums with us."

"Ohh." So, what am I supposed to do?? Salute & wish 'congratulations' on this proud victory, sir.

"What do you have to say about that??"

"Was that your idea?"

"Uhm, sort of. What do you say about it?"

"How can you just bring anyone in '5th ace'?? I mean they are from 'Vishesh', our opponents." I asked.

"'Our opponents'? But that was past, right. I can bring them because that is what I need to do at this point of time." giving an afterthought, he added. "..and we have decided to give a new name to our band."

"Oh great then."

"C'mon sir, don't tell me now that's going to hurt you." He said in his newly acquired accent.

"Why would that be?? Ajit, Do me a slight favor, tell me that the motive behind this call??"

"I'm calling to inform that you can come and play keyboard in the band, if you want." He told me, as the arrogance of his words echoed in my ears.

"If you want????" I asked him bluntly, to answer Mr. Bossy.

"I just mean do come, if you are able to manage stuff."

"That might not be possible, at least so far. I need to go right now." I told him. I did not feel aggrieved on Ajit, neither badly shocked. I had seen better chameleons than him in the past few years that I had lived. Success is tough for some guys to handle, and Ajit was just being one of them. Thinking of going back to play with him was out of question.

Two days later, Anshul called me. Before I picked up, I hoped not to hear from him in the high-headed kind of way Ajit had recently acquired. Thankfully, god did not turn my hopes down this time.

"Sir, Ajit had called you to invite you." Anshul said in a tone soft as always.

"Oh, he did, if we invite people by talking in that manner."

"I'm really sorry for his behaviour. But he is like that now-a-days, but sir we discussed that it would be great to have you even if it is for a short span."

"Look, Anshul, I really don't know what made you guys unite with Jatin. Even when both of you know that...."I stopped amid of my sentence.

"It was Ajit's contemplation sir, I knew that action could pinch you but please, if you can try and ignore all this."

"Not that easy, I guess."

"Hmm. Sir, I request you to come & practice with us, please."

"Don't say please man. But I can't manage to bear Jatin's presence around at all. "

"Sir, I'm requesting you to come on my & Ajit's behalf. Jatin & Dinesh are least involved. And even after you come, you'll not need to talk to him. Treat like he does not exist, we would not mind. But do come please, Will you??"

I could not say 'no' to Anshul after he convinced me.

"Hmmm, I'll."

I had my I-card, so it was not tough to enter the college. Yes, it was against the rules. But my motive was not wrong. They say music flows without boundaries, I was just moving along, so it was not my fault. We started practicing after college timings, but seeing Jatin & Dinesh playing with us, could not be called a feast for my eyes.

To be honest, I did not give a damn for the new drummer. Jatin was the one who made me remember of things, of Ameesh, & of VISHESH. On his part, he too stole eyes from me. Meanwhile all this, Ajit was on his own trip, doing whatever he could, without consulting both of us.

"So, you have even selected the songs. Have you??" Anshul asked him, throwing a disgusted look.

He even chose our new band mates without telling us, I wanted to say.

It is weird to find someone you know from so long in a shade you hardly expect from them. It was Indeed, Ajit's darkest shade. His attitude & body language was so changed, that even the way he talked to me over phone seemed way more polite for him. A glint of obstinacy seemed to sparkle in his eyes every time he opened up.

Ajit announced to us "I'd play lead guitar this time".

I nodded while listening to the newly emerged commandant. Unfortunately, that did not mark an end to his domination. Whenever we jammed, his attitude began to put everything else in shade. He was hardly willing to listen to anyone else's suggestions, whether they come from Anshul or from me.

I was playing the keyboard once, when he started poking his nose. "Ughh. Change this tone, it is not coming right."

"That's sounding shitty, better play it like this." He would say & play any random tone that his heart liked, irrespective of whether it was relevant in the song or not.

He did all that he could to raise my heckles. Who was he to treat us like 'beast of burden'?

The water had risen above my head, and it needed to be brought down at the soonest. His sense of superiority was getting too tough to be handled. My ego, my self-respect called me names, while I tried to bear Ajit & stay there, putting my patience at drills every day. So that was when my endurance gave up. So I texted him one day, after coming back home:

Thanks for the chance, sir, but I would not be lucky enough to join your band.

That was the last day when I went to practice with them.

It was mid of September, when I received my joining letter from TCS I had the offer letter but my wait for the joining letter was meant to evaporate that day.

"Joining date: March 29th, 2012 & joining venue: Ahmadabad"

I read the line again. That smile over my face began to fade away in no time. I mean yes, Ahmadabad was a great city, lots that I've heard about it, but 29th march???? Have they been kidding?? But why would they be??

It was expected to be in October or November utmost. Is march an error?? Of course, it could not be. But what would I do, for 7 long months that were lined up before me?? Watch TV. , kill time on chatting, or count stars?? May be all of them together.

I was posing questions to myself. I was answering them by myself. That's how you are likely to react when you are watching a nightmare with eyes wide open. But how come it be so soon, oops so late?? I was not even in my senses. I counted the remaining months for another time at my fingers, but it did not help in reducing the number. The wait did not get any less, it prolonged even more.

I decided to shut down the computer so that it did not piss me off more. After a few minutes, Pulkit told me that we shared the joining date& the venue as well. It made me feel better. A lot better. Owing to my minds fondness for sheer optimism, I began to figure out the possible advantages of what had just passed over me, rather than feeling miserable about it.

Killing time at home provoked my brain & flooded in it new schemes every now & then. The teaching interviews were over, the call centre's were not my spot of interest. And of course, if I may say so, the 5th ace was at its exploitation.

Once I was surfing over net, when I saw an advertisement on knowafest.com about "Battle of Bands" event in some college. It transported me to the world where my band the '5th ace' once existed. I thought of talking to Anshul but he could hardly be able to do much in Jatin's presence, I knew. I would not call Ajit for sure, I knew, since he was not the same. Neither would my ego doing anything of that sort.

It took one complete day to make up my mind and I called up the Sameer. I was aware that I could be the last man alive who Sameer would list among his favourites. He was thoroughly justified if he shuns me off after what I did with him, but a part of my heart said 'he won't.' And that I could rely on him. But I lost all the hope as he disconnected the call. It is amazing to me how one click is enough to crush one's hopes. Perhaps, he too did not want to talk to someone who never believed in him.

Yes, I deserved all this owing to my deeds. At some point or another, I had to pay for them. I forgot about the fest and tried to get involved in to something else. After an hour or so, my phone rang up, 'Sameer calling' flashed.

"Hey sir, I was in the lecture, so I disconnected the phone call." His words sounded magical to me. They say, god has his own ways to make the unexpected come true all the time.

Unlike many others, his feet were still grounded on earth "It is ok, Sameer. I did not realize that college is not over for everyone."

"Yep, but it'll someday. Anyways, how have you been all these days?"

"Pretty fine." I said. 'Pretty idle' was the truth.

"So, when will you be joining TCS??" he asked me.

"Well, I'm looking forward to it, but they seem to be in no hurry. The joining date is 29th march."

"Ohh really?? That is a lot of time in hand."

"Yea, I guess I'm destined to attend our college fest for the 5th time." I chuckled.

"I agree to that note."

"Sameer, I wanted to know about your band's progress. Have you guys found a lead guitarist??"

"Sadly no. In fact, that's what keeps me bothering, but we are praying to find one soon."

Then, I told him about the advertisement I saw for the inter-college fest organized at S.B.I.T. College, Sonepat.

He became excited on hearing that and said "sounds good. I suppose my friends would be interested too."

"Certainly. Sameer, I wanted to know about something else too. Am I... am I still eligible to play guitar in 'Moksha'?? " I asked him, my fingers crossed and my heartbeat began to race up. Sameer said a word the very next moment, which I failed to hear. Perhaps, I had gone deaf with anxiety.

"Pardon please." I said.

"Sir, that has to be a 'yes'. Of course you are." He said, his clear words comforting me for the first time in last 2 months. This is about life; people who are hardly given care surprise you by helping in every way, when the world turns its back at you.

I was called to practice with 'Moksha' within 3 days of my call. Though I had initiated it very keenly, but things were not going to be that easy, I thought. Seeing that Moksha did have people other than just Sameer, I was a bit unsure. After all, I could not deny that I was a left-out stranger for them. I wondered if I would be able to fall in sync with them.

I wondered if they'll be able to adjust with a wild card entry in their band. What if they take it as an intervention? And worse, if they are unconvinced and refuse to accept me in their band?? People like Ajit, Jatin, and many others will get another reason to prove they were so right. And that I was not. Maybe I was thinking too much but all these were the last thing that I was wishing to turn into reality. I made up my mind to go up for practice, leaving everything else up to god.

I was eager to go to the college after such a long time, as I looked forward to developments taking place in life. By god's grace, no Ameesh, no Rohit, no Manav to tolerate. College has to be newer, and greater without some of those anti-Aryan elements, I convinced myself hard to get out of the bed that Saturday morning. Getting out of bed is always painful, no matter what.

Quite unsurprisingly, Sameer had rung me up to remind me that I had to turn up at the practice floor with Moksha. I bet he would top the university, if 'responsibility' was a part of our course.

Head held high, I entered into the gate that led me to the place where I had spent the most memorable part of my life, the College. More or less, my mind was clouded with all the possible imaginations of what could be lined up before as I walked through those corridors. Sameer's band-mates were with him, as I arrived at their practice room. After he got me introduced to the other to band members, we played some music. Sameer realized that being an alumnus, I'm not allowed to visit college on regular basis & practice in the premises, so they sought the director's permission the next day.

At the practice sessions, things were in contrast to all the bad things I thought could happen, thankfully. I jumped into 'MOKSHA' later than everyone else, but got comfortable very soon. In fact, I had never been more relieved playing as a part of a band. Their behavior never made me feel alienated, not even for a minute. It is amazing how everything you expect is turned down by the reality that lies ahead. If you expect bad, all the good things come running to knock your door, and of course the vice versa.

More sessions of practice with the 'Moksha' made me realize that I could confide my ideas with them just like everybody else & they valued it. Things were merry again with the 'craziest sort of guys' I had seen under JMIT's roof. The fest that we were preparing for was 20 days away. So, we moved heavens and earth to succeed with music. We prepared a nice and contenting 17-minutes shot to perform at the stage.

22nd 0ctober 2011, SBIT.

Though the city of Sonepat was 100km's away, we managed to reach SBIT on time. "The 3rd band is about to perform." I said, my eyes still on the stage, but mind clouded by thoughts. Ours was going to be the next turn. And it was perplexing. After so many hurdles, rifts, adjustments, the moment had finally arrived. We were minutes short of performing what we have given a whole month.

Everybody was speaking whatever was running in their mind. They were nervous too, but I had always been the extreme case, no matter what. Let alone performing in some other college, I was performing another time, something I least expected turning into reality months ago. If something could release me from this unease, it was playing music to that wonderful audience. Only that! Thankfully, we were called at the stage in no time.

Things at SBIT's stage were quite different. In fact, much better! They had done everything required to help a performer in living up to his best. During the sound check, there was nothing except darkness. But the very second, we started playing it looked like all the lights of the city had been brought to focus on Sameer. May be, if Ajit would have been at his place, I would not have been an inch happier as much I was for Sameer. But this was 'Moksha', not an iota of envy!

Sameer's confidence boosted up. And it showed well in his voice. It was as radiant as we could ever imagine. When I started playing my solo, the lights came onto me. It was something, man! I mean, being at the spot light in mid of thousand people. That ray of light was enough to bring one of the widest smiles at my face. I was ECSTATIC.

The lights dimmed and brightened up in nanoseconds. As the performance continued, it gleamed on the rest on our mates and the crowd went at top of its spirits. Sameer went ahead on the ramp and talked to audiences whenever we switched the songs. On my end I was performing for the first time. There a difference between playing and performing. I played in my own college. At SBIT, I was performing, giving my best, relating with the audience.

And Kanav the great was gone with the wind. If that stud smile was not enough, he was shaking his head along with the tone, catching every possible attention. As he came towards my side for crossing the guitars, I dreaded if I would end up laughing my lungs out. The crowd was in love with it. The wobbling of heads spread among them. We still call it the 'Kanav Virus'. They were lively as hell. We performed and they roared.

I wonder whether it was the hardships that we had to face before, the glowing ambience or the lovely audiences that pepped us up. Just as we finished the sensational crowd shouted 'once more, once more'. I realized for what I strived through all. That was the best any performer can feel.

That night, while we were packing to come back, Sameer walked up to me & said, "sir, the performance has got finished, but I hope it is not the end, but a starting that I always wanted to begin with." My lips curved into a wide smile & I nodded.

After the SBIT Show, we were all at the seventh heaven. The performance did not fell an inch shorter than we expected. Talking about the experience we had, brought a smile at my face. It gave a sense of content & pride. We uploaded videos & dropped status on facebook sharing our happiness.

I don't know for how many times I, particularly, saw the performance video. And every time I saw them I felt joyous. A month passed. Meanwhile our practice continued after the college hours. We began to be recognized as a 'band' by many people now.

The month of November was at its closing stages. We had decided to allay the practice sessions for some days since it was exams season again. Till then, I had become a part of their band, an equally important part.

'I.I.L.M.' College, situated in Gurgaon, was organizing an inter-college fest, I saw at knowafest.com. I was a bit hesitant in the beginning since it was exams season. Ruining your responsibility for the sake of your passion is nonsensical. But, I called up Sameer and Kanav to ask when their semester exams were supposed to begin. Only after they told that they had to be utmost one and a half month away, I told them about the fest. On hearing the news, they were unstoppable. After we talked to Punit, our next voyage got a start.

The city was nowhere close to ours, but geographical conditions are capable to reduce our passion for bringing music in to action. We prepared 5 songs for the upcoming fest with all the zeal. Our desperation for music made us overcome a lot many hurdles.

Yes, I might lose my job after this, my college could be putting me behind the bars after admitting this, or my own 'MOKSHA' friends might come & kill me for letting the secret out, but we forged authority signatures & official stamps too. We did. Given that the semester was on its closing stages, we knew that the college would not grant us the permission. The ignition to play on the stage made us do that. May be that's why they say, Forbidden fruit tastes the best.

The final day, 2nd Dec,2011 soon came to us flying. The 7-hr long journey meant that travelling down by a bus was not a choice, but the only option in front of us. Moreover, taking a car or riding on bikes to the destination might do no less than burning a hole in our pockets. We had decided to depart by 8 in the morning, not taking any risks.

Everything got paid as we reached 'IILM' on the reporting time. We were desperate to repeat SBIT's success by hook or by crook. The show began at around 8 p.m.. Pretty confident this time, we were enjoying. By default, we had got the second last slot to perform.

4 bands performed on the stage & the 3rd last one's arrival was announced. We were called backstage within seconds. Thinking that our performance was just a few minutes away, a sense of nervousness started stirring up in us. S.B.I.T turned out to be fun. But once you do well, pressure builds up to keep that going. We had to get serious in the now-or-never situation.

"Hey, guys. There is a bit change in the schedule." the IILM guy came & told us. He added that our performance has been shifted to the last slot.

It was strange to see them changing their mind at the end moment. But last turn was not bad either. It meant an extra benefit to make the performance a big hit, so we did not question anything from the ordering authority. We nodded & smiled at him.

"Alright then, good luck." The 3rd last band & IILM's performance wrapped up, we were called on the stage.

At stage, the things always look different. Every time seems to be the first time, no matter how long you have been running in the race. Elated we were. However, the happiness was short-lived & survived just for a couple of moments. It got murdered as the sound check began.

After Punit complained, we figured out that the Drum pedal was in a pathetic condition. He tried considerable number of times, but the beat sucked. Every time he beat against the drums, we feared the pedal would get smashed.

We all understood, what made the organizers change their mind. We were offered to play at the last position and it was not luck, but ill-luck. To worse, the audience looked dismal. The crowd had almost got vanished, adding more to our misery. This time, our performance depended on things other than our caliber. We had absolutely no idea of what would become of us. A crash or a soar? While we were fidgeting with thoughts in our head, we were asked to start the performance soon.

We hardly had any alternative other than praying that the pedal's condition does not get worse. Our hearts sank but the presence of mind made us perform. And do at least our part. Whosoever said, it's the mind that ruins it all was, not a genius.

We decided to perform, but could not manage to do more than 3 songs. Forget about 'once more', the people applauded like it was a punishment. Performing at 10:30, under those cold waves, was getting least manageable.

Half-heartedly performed, we stepped down from the stage within 9 minutes. It was not one of the most enjoyable encounters with music for us, to say the least. Neither the most memorable one. And it was too late to mend anything. On the way back, all hopes fell apart. The past few hours seemed like they were an outcome of a curse. Gloom had replaced satisfaction. Our faces were sunk as much as our spirits were.

All we wanted was to get someone who could tell us it was a scary nightmare, and not a final performance. Yes, it felt pathetic. But we knew we had to put a brave face. We tried every bit to cheer each other. 'No blame games' is Moksha's forte! We stood by each other, when it was needed the most. And that's what counts I guess.

My band mates got busy with their semester exams. There were no practice sessions, so I tried to immerse myself in a schedule that persisted when college went for me. It actually was no schedule, no agenda, but a program that offered a variety of ways to murder time.

Luckily, the wait for joining got lessened, when January ended. I was happy to assume that we could go back to the practices & performances, since the exams got over too. But I did get disappointed when they informed me that companies were coming for placements, the next fortnight. It meant we'd to hold the fire for a few more days. Of course, it was not a too big a price, if it comes to someone's career.

Surprisingly, some of the juniors did ring me up on rare occasions to ask for some guidelines about placements. My selection in 'TCS' had made them aware of the fact that looks could be deceptive. And I could not be called really bad at academics by any measure. In my four years of engineering, not many people in flesh knew I had this silent disease of becoming 'studious' types every 2 months per year. But no matter what day it is, I could not bear any confusion about my academic status.

However, there used to be one girl who always figured out this part of me, Sirat. Despite of all the sad things that made way between us, I could never deny being indebted to her, for the helping hand she had extended in my placement days. If I had a job in my hands before college ended, she played a significant role in it. I could hardly remember or imagine her criticizing one thing about me, even when the world between us got upside down.

It seems funny, when your mind starts using phrases like 'used-to-be', when your heart lingers on that thing. Every time a junior would ask me about some advice, it would make me remember of her.

Deep inside my heart, I had a longing desire that she too would call me up a day or another to ask about the course, or about the selection tests, or about anything. But she never did. Of course, she would prefer someone less egoistic to ask for some advice. I wanted to ask her about the preparations, time and again. But that thing called 'Why-should-I' EGO never allowed me to do that.

What tomorrow might bring…

One night, I was lying on my bed lazily, when the message tone of my cell-phone beeped. Like most of the time, I ignored, thinking the cell-phone won't run away anywhere. After 15 minutes, I saw a message in the inbox.

It was a 'Good night.' Wish from Sirat. I tried to resist, but I texted her back.

Good night, how have you been??

The next second, my phone buzzed again. She replied back:

I'm fine.

Yeah, just that. I texted her back: TCS is coming right??

Yes, sir. On this 12th itself, how are you??

I'm doing fine. So, how are the preparations going??

She replied back:

I'm working hard, so let's see what happens. And by the way, you are still not allowed to say 'thanks'.

Reading her reply helped me put a genuine smile on my face. It said that I still meant more than a 'stranger' to her.

I replied back:

Of course, Sirat. And you'll, I know. Wanted to say please, don't feel shy from asking if you need some help.

To that, she replied:

Sure. But you have already helped me a lot. Through our discussions before your own placements, it is helping me.

I re-read the text again. I re-read the 1st line again & again. I wondered if the first line of her text pointed to something else. Was she taunting on me, by saying that?? No, she was not, I thought. At least, I knew her that much.

I replied back, "That's good. And do tell me, When the sun shines at you too.

She replied back:

Undoubtedly, I would love to. I'll rush back to my books now, if you don't mind..

I replied back:

"You better do that: p just kidding. Go ahead. Good night."

My phone beeped for the last time that night.

"Good night. Take care"

12-february-2012 brought me the good news that - Kanav too had got placed in 'TCS'. Optimistic, that I was, I felt delighted to know that the journey for music would not halt after college. Although, things did not turn out well for Sameer & Punit, I wished that they could hit the success very soon. And then, I wondered what happened about Sirat.

I had texted her wishing 'Good luck'. & She had replied saying 'Thanks' but there were no signs of her even when the placement session were over. No text, no calls even hours later. Some cynical thoughts did try to enter my mind, but I shoved them away thinking she would be busy.

That evening, Sirat called me. "I've got selected too." She announced with elation in her voice.

"Great!!!! Congratulations." I told her. Though I never told her but I was confident that she would, from the first moment. We talked for two minutes more. And she hung up the phone. I was happy that at least, her luck was not treating her ruthlessly in the way I did.

Finally, the placement drive was over. For me, it meant commencement of the 'passion' spell once again. We started practicing again. We had heard that 'N.C. COLLEGE, Israna' was going to celebrate the fest. The real bonanza was 10,000 was the reserved cash prize for the winning side. They had asked to send a video of the interested bands. We took no time to mail them a nice one. Also, they were quick enough to respond in positive.

Being registered, we pulled up our socks to give our best shot. Apart from 4 songs, we had even composed a song by ourselves. 'Khudgarzi' was our first original composition. It was going to be my 3rd performance with them. And the past two had made aware that the one of the major reason behind my compatibility with 'Moksha' was the resemblance of opinions about songs too.

As per our plan, we traversed to Israna on our bikes this time. It took just 3 hours to reach our destiny. We reached the college on time & asked for a safe 3rd last slot to perform. Our expedition to Gurgaon had taught us that a good performance does not need a specific slot to get appreciated by the audience. But backstage, we were worried to some extent. The crash at 'IILM' terrified us. Finally the call was made on the stage. We went on the stage forgetting what we did in SBIT, and trying to forget what happened with us in IILM.

Close to six, dusk was about to fall when we went on the stage. But there's no fun like performing in the dark. So, we had planned to take extra time for the sound check to delay our performance. We wanted to take complete benefit of NC College's lightening system. It was not unfair. Fortunately, it worked.

After the 20minutes-long sound check, music went into action and we obeyed. The phobia inside us evaporated as Sameer's voice filled the venue. With every moment, our confidence boosted up, making us do better. The picture perfect lights contributed in making the performance a feast for ears as well as eyes. The songs made the crowd go mad with ecstasy. It was the ultimate view for all of us. The audience pepped us to keep on performing. We had set the stage on fire.

Though we completed those 5 songs, but even after that it seemed as if we have just stepped up on the stage a moment ago. Perhaps, the captivating audience was responsible for making us believe that. They even roared for 'once more'. But we had to come down. We had enjoyed ours, but it was time for others to perform. Not to forget, NC's huge ground was something to remember.

Back stage, everybody came running towards us. People shook hands with us. Unbelievingly, a group of girls even asked for a photograph with all of us. With MOKSHA. We got it clicked. Even though we did not win the competition, we were zenith of happiness. We were satisfied.

Back at home, we were stars. Facebook, like always, behaved as the messenger of our success .Every passing moment made me contented that I was living my passion. An evening when I logged into my facebook account, I received an unusual text in my inbox. To be honest, it was usual text from an unpredicted person.

"Hiii."

"Hiii Rohit." I replied. Yes, we had added each other in our accounts but that was years ago, almost 4 years ago, when we had just jumped in to the college. However, I could not remember if we had ever had a chat since that day, since we were never exactly on amiable terms.

"How are you?"

"I'm fine."

"Hmm, how's life?? Music happening there, I suppose??"

"Yup. " I had decided to keep it short rather than entertaining him with affection-loaded replies.

"So I heard you have mingled up with some band called……" he replied back. Though, I was not interested to talk to him on this particularly, but I wrote back.

"Moksha. I'm performing with Moksha."

"Found that from the videos."

"Ok." I thought of asking if he liked them so as to add up to the conversation, but then I chucked the idea when his images of past spun in my head. He did not reply for a couple of minutes, giving me a sigh of relief. There he was finally, the impulsive Rohit.

"So, I was talking to Jatin another day and he told me you went to practice for a day and then turned a back at them. Now, a silent rift with the 5th Ace?" oh wow, so it's been almost 8 months that college ended, but still I was the unrivaled topic of their gossips.

A lot was running in my mind to write back to his reply, but I finally wrote, "Not rift; I was occupied with other things, so preferred not to continue with them."

"How believable is that." He answered taking a dig at me.

"Excuse me."

"I know what the actual scene is."

"Ok." I said, hoping he would not prod anymore.

"I could guess that easily."

Now what was that?? Excuse me for being rude, but in no way, I considered myself answerable to this disgusting jerk, who had played his part well enough in messing up things for me.

"'Easily'? What do you want to convey?" I replied back, holding the string of patience.

"Nothing." He wrote back.

And then I got another text from him that said:

"Let me give you some advice. Buddy, grow up. And change your 'fight-blame-revenge game' attitude that you master at. It has not led you anywhere in the past 4 years. And believe me; it won't let you go any far, if you cling to it. Forget other things, you'll not be able to survive within this 'MOKSHA', if you don't mend your ways. Trust me on that."

Now that was some real attitude, was it not? My dearest friend was back to his true face. With a bang. Nobody, I ever came across in 20 years of my life, could rival him (READ: along with Manav) in being intolerant. For next 30 seconds, I continued staring at the chunk of attitude posted in my inbox, calmed myself down and then wrote back.

"Great Rohit, what a sage advice. I can feel being indebted to your concern. But one thing if I can ask you to do… For heaven's sake, stop interfering in other people's life. Just spare me for whatever I do in my life.".

“This ego is exactly what I’m talking about. This self-obsessed attitude has made a home in your thick-headed brain.”

“For god’s sake, try & not bother for that.”

“Ohh please, pardon me, if you think I’m even interested in doing that. What makes you that by giving some performances, you can compete with us. Who does not know that it has been your aim, just because you could not make up to ‘Vishesh’?”

“It is amazing to me you consider yourself that important. I’m afraid to disappoint you brother, but I do have better things to do than your idle brain can imagine.”

“Oh really, As If I’ll believe you said the truth.”

“For hell’s sake, Can you understand that I don’t give a damn about whether you believe it or not?”

“Whatever, in Jmit’s eyes, you have lost it time and again, that’s what matters. Bear one thing in mind, just performing once or twice would not make you a ‘hero’. Bye. ”

Just as I read those lines, I could imagine him spanking that hard on my face. I tried and wrote uncountable number of answers, but none made enough sense.

Only after my burning insides settled a bit, I managed to send him, keeping up the sarcasm,

“And of course, thank you for the lovely advice, bye.”

I removed him from my facebook account before I logged off that night. His words kept ringing in my head, bringing to me, and countless number of questions. Did I need to prove anything to someone yet, I wondered. Did it still make a difference to me? Was he right when he said that people at my college would barely remember the time I performed? Was something necessary still left for me to do? All this questions sprinted in my head and I tried running away from the truth. But, I was no more a kind who could stir his mind elsewhere. There was only 1 answer to all of the question marks. It was a Yes.

March 1, 2012.

I had finally entered the month when I'll be joining at my job. The month that would take me away from here, the month that would transport me to another state, a city that I had never seen before. The month that I had been waiting for so long.

It was also the month in which my college used to organize its annual fest, not my college actually. It would be the last opportunity for me to attend it, if I could make it possible this time. I'd be leaving at this 28th. So all my hopes hinged on the dates decided for the fest.

I was desperate to perform, in front of my own college one more time. Also, many people around me needed a gunshot, and a nice performance could serve the purpose equally well, I knew.

The convocation ceremony was always meant to be on the first day of the fest. If only it is scheduled on 27th or before, things would work. I prayed them to work. But my hopes turned into disappointment, when I got to know that the college scheduled the fest on 2nd and 3rd April.

I had realized that apart from prayers, plans were needed too. So, I laid a plan. Like me, some 52 students of our batch too had their joining by the end of the march. May be this fact could be put in to use, I thought. I had to make this count.

I logged on to the college's website & swirled to find out the list of those students. Many of them were big-headed, high-noses. But I did contact a few of them, who looked appropriate enough to understand. I phone-called whoever I could. And I mailed others suggesting that our requests might make them to pre-pone the convocation ceremony. If it was my convocation, it was their too? And which idiot on earth would like to miss that day, I thought. All that they needed to do was making a call to the Director or send an e-mail.

The fact, that it could help, did register in to some minds. But some of them remained skeptical.

"Why they would care to pre-pone it for the bunch of 50 students", they said.

They might not, but a mail would do no harm, I told them back. I asked everyone to ask their friends if they could get involve too. On my part, I had called the college authorities from every phone-number that I had access to.

I asked some of my junior friends to talk to the organizing committee & convey that their seniors were waiting for their degree to get in hands. Luckily, they agreed to help me willingly. Honestly, convincing them to do that was a way easier than asking the snobs of my own class. I called them once to know if the plea's had borne any fruit & they had changed their minds. Fortunately, the good news came flying over to us.

The college has rescheduled the convocation & the fest on 27th, and 28th march respectively, the heavy voice on the other side said. But to me, what mattered was not actually the convocation ceremony. The fest was the real reason behind.

I did not want to miss it, and I could not afford to miss the first day of my job too. In the war between responsibility & passion, I had finally found a mid-way. Destiny helped me in resorting back to life, when I was informed that the morning of 27th was reserved march for the Convocation ceremony. And in the evening, the battle of bands event was scheduled.

Meanwhile, mom at home announced that I should start collecting things now. I began shopping with her, to getting the requirements. I was going to join the corporate world. So, it meant that I could not hang around my office, wearing my denim jeans & tees. It was time to make formals wear a way of life. I had to buy shirts, and trousers. Like every other guy, I hated shopping, but I could not run away this time. She said that she did not want me to make any compromises. I brought the other necessities too. Shoes, sleepers, 1 blanket, prescribed medicines, everything.

In the college, the preparations of fest had started. Sameer had given me a call, asking me to come along for the practice session. We started practicing together all over again. Just 11days were left for the fest & 12 for my departure. So, I had to cope up between preparations of the two. I had to get some necessary documentation done before joining at the work place. And now, all of a sudden, the time seemed to sprint away like a brook. I managed doing all the things before the timings set for jamming.

The days had got divided into 2 parts: at college and back from college. The way it was for last 4 years. But only that it was at the finishing edge. The years of my stay at the beautiful place were at their closing stage.

Life, however, was turning out to be hectic in order to organize everything. With my tight schedule, It got hard to spare a second giving a thought to anything else. The last mile is always the hardest, they say it so right.

Our experience had now made it easy for us to find a tune for all of us. We had prepared swiftly 6 songs, in just 9 days.

27th March, 2012

Sunlight broke in to my bedroom. My gaze fell upon the clock hung at the wall facing me. It was close to 10 O'clock. I looked around to find mom packing my luggage and sobbing. I got really mush up looking at the tears falling down her face.

"What happened mumma?? Where are dad and Ishu?" I asked her. She did not answer.

I asked her again and prayed not to get any of the terrible answer that my mind had begun thinking of.

"Your dad has gone to work and Ishu's left for college."

"Then what is wrong mumma??"

She wiped her tears and said "nothing." I tried asking her the reason behind the tears, but she kept mum. After a minute, she looked at me & broke up again.

"Tell me, why are you crying??" it was getting harder to see her in that condition.

"You'll leave tomorrow." she said fighting a lump in her throat.

"Won't you??" That was all she said. One statement by her made everything clear. I could see her dilemma at least, if not able to understand it.

"I'll have to, but that's for a job." I said tried to soothe her.

"Hmmm. I know." She said, trying not to weep more.

"So, you are sad & want me to stay??"

"Of course not stupid, which mother on earth would want her son to stop from progressing." She said gaining her senses. Thank god.

"That's it. And c'mon, I'll come home whenever it would possible." I told her. She nodded, with belief in her eyes. I was relieved that she was not crying now.

"But you are so lil right now, I fear that you'll have to fight alone in a totally different world." It made me laugh to see her behaving like a kid now. I wondered how I had switched places with her, that too overnight

"Mumma, it is not a battle ground and your lil boy has completed his engineering now."

"I know Aryan, but..." .

"Don't worry, I'm not going to any desert." I said, as Mumma nodded. Her expression worried me a bit, but I did not give up.

"I'll call you twice every day." I continued. It took me some time but she got cheered up. Her smile returned back. That flawless dimple that I had got from her flashed too. It suited her more than anyone else.

After a bit of consolation & lots of 'I-will-take-care' promises to mom, I took bath and got ready for my convocation ceremony. By the time I reached college, I had already received 2 calls from Pulkit.

I had heard more than once that days like your convocation ceremony bring you your best memories & leave you with the most cherished experiences life can ever offer. Memories of the times that I lost long back to the hands of past rushed back, just as I came face to face with them all. With my batch-mates!

They are the category of people who never failed to surprise me. I could not have expected my classmates to be so warm till that day was held. When I was hating to see those sore faces, I found them screaming for amity. And I was dumbstruck by what I got, sheer friendliness. I mean, were those smiles for real?

If they are not saints, they are not really wicked. A few of them not at all wicked. I kept this repeating in my mind. It helped me reciprocate the politeness that existed in the air around us. The grudges looked replaced with embraces, even if it was for just one day. We resembled like siblings (Couples excuse!) who had reunited after life-long partitions.

And all of a sudden, all the good times that we had shared on this part of the planet clouded my mind, putting all the frictions into shade. May be this is called growing up & settling down.

Just one sight of each other, and a million stories were ready to get discussed, laughed out. And the most thrilling part, our degree. I mean was anything more worth than wearing those robs, which had the power to entice one for as long as 4 years. Rohit & Ameesh were also there....

Quite unexpectedly, Ameesh turned up to me with a smiling face. As he started conversing politely, I wondered if I could do any good to him. That tone in which he spoke made me remember of the way he was 4 years ago when we were friends or I assumed that we were so.

He mentioned about the performance videos that I had uploaded. He congratulated me about our success at 'SBIT'. He said that he was happy that finally my efforts were getting paid. On my part, I did not shove him away, giving a cold shoulder. I reciprocated back the same amity that he displayed.

After he left, I thought about Ameesh. About every other person who had cut me down, who used to say that I was building castles in air! And how they are coming to pat my back now? I had finally done fidelity to the promise I had made to myself to prove them wrong.

So finally, I had to make ridiculous faces at least at one person less. But Rohit? His coming was never a pleasure. It could never be.

Before Pulkit left I asked him, "Hey, you're coming in the evening, right?"

"How can I not? Of course, I'm." Pulkit said. I smiled back and walked to the practice room to prepare for the performance I was longing for.

The battle of bands was scheduled at 6:30 p.m., so I returned back home at 4 O'clock to change my attire.

As I sat in the veranda of my house, thoughts about the evening that stood firm in front of me flood my mind. How is it going to be? How every one of us has prepared for it? I would give up my all to this performance a grand success. I wanted but what if something screws us up?? What if everything gets scattered at the end moment?? I tried to shove away the negative thoughts coming in to my mind.

I thought of packing things. But dropped the idea, thinking it would make me feel worse. Plus, it would increment mom's job making it double, first unpacking & then packing up in the right manner.

I diverted my mind, and thought about what to wear. Possibly the last performance in my college, I had to look good in any case. I had worn a black shirt last time, so black was not on the list this time. With some struggle, I settled on a white shirt & blue denims. I left for college soon after.

Pulkit, like he promised, reached college on time. And along with him there was one more guy arrived. Rohit!!

"What fallen in love?" Pulkit mocked at me, as I looked back Rohit in shock. His mere sight made me inconvenient.

"Yeah, why not? How come he is here?" I asked Pulkit, as we walked away.

"Why can't he?" Pulkit said.

"Speak up, man or I'll get you killed right here."

"He said that he'll be leaving….." He said, keeping up the suspense, as I rolled my eyes. "..Tomorrow morning. He'll catch the same train as I'm. So, he stayed back to watch the fest. You better enjoy in your flight."

"Detailed info." I chuckled.

"Best friends you know." Pulkit said, as we laughed mutedly.

'Moksha' were called out along with the 3 other participating bands. We saw the performances begun. Ours was the last one. At the backstage, I saw things around me. How different they looked after one year. A year before, I was there as a student. There were floods of people who I knew, people who knew me. Tonight, only a few of them were left. I looked at my band-mates. Undoubtedly, the best guys I came across in my college life.

I looked at Sameer. My favourite singer ever. His serious expressions were unforgettable. Even though he was years younger, I respected him a lot. In fact, he was the reason I was here today.

I looked at Punit. Even his habit of saying 'Hai na Hai na' at the end of every statement, & his pouting expression, when we did not agree. He was the kid. Harmless. Inoffensive.

I looked at Kanav. His poor jokes now seemed funny. In 21years of my life till then, I had not come across a guy who hated rules more than Kanav did. Crystal hearted people, they were. They had taught me a lot. To bend. To relive music. To believe. In them, in myself too. Nothing would have been possible without them.

The announcers called out MOKSHA to do the action. After we made a final word, we went at the stage, to satisfy our thirst. I was excited, for it was going to be the last time. But it never meant that rest of my mates felt ease. After the sound check, our performance started. We had made sure that our performance included every kind of song. We began with an emotional song, which could potentially touch hearts. It did, the applause made it evident.

I looked up at the crowd searching for Rohit and saw faces enjoying. I could not find him anywhere. Even that made me happy. Destiny had finally made us switch places. Tonight, I was performing and he was lost in the crowd. Revenge is sweet, isn't it? If he could see my face, it won't take him much to figure out I was on the top of the world where happiness ruled.

After a while, I recognized one of them. A girl sitting exactly in front of me, behind 5-6 rows. I saw Sirat. From the spot I was standing at, she was clearly visible. She was looking at me too. She moved away eyes, breaking our gaze. We marched further with a song from the movie 'rockstar', and then an old melody. The naughty lines made the crowd roar. The crowd was enjoying. I wished Rohit notice that all, and that I could see him, and his face becoming red with envy. But he was nowhere to be seen. People at back even stood on their chairs. It was thunder magic Life.

Just as our performance ended, the crowd demanded "once more". Surprisingly, the girls' side screamed even louder. The announcers asked us to perform one more song for the compelling audiences. Well, who would not want to? I could not resist looking where Sirat was sitting. Again, I might not see her again in life. Ever!

After 25 long minutes of live stardom, we came down from the stage. Feeling what I felt in those moments was the aim of my life, not a mere objective. I had lived my dream. The longing desire was finally fulfilled. The applauses echoed in my ears.

The next moment, Pulkit hugged me, and praised our performance. Also, he made Rohit listen to each and every word of the appraisal. Rohit's presence evoked an urge in me. I wanted to tell him how much I had waited for this moment to come.

If it was in my hands, I would not see that face again. Yes, under no circumstances. But things were different tonight, I was happier than anyone else that he stayed back. I was happy that life offered a moment when I performed, he was lost among the crowd being just another face in hundreds. Year after year, he had worked so hard to make me feel creepy. And now, it was my turn to reciprocate him back. He was one of the driving forces that made our performance be that good.

I drove back to home, with that smiling face & guitar at my back. After coming back home at 10, I had dinner with my family. They had been waiting for me to return. It was not usual but I guess they too did not want to miss any second that the four of us could spend together. Mum, dad, Ishu, and me.

I arranged the left-over. And put the documents that were to be taken along, in order. Each one had its own story. I packed my guitar & keyboard, and kept them inside the cupboard. Life would be such a mistake without them, I thought. How badly I wanted to take them along with me. How pitifully I could not. I was going to miss them the most, I knew from day one.

I fidgeted with my phone & managed to text a few numbers in the contact list. I wrote a message indicating that I would be leaving for Ahmadabad the next morning. Another way of telling that I would not be able to attend the chit-chatting calls from now.

I was exhausted as hell, but that night when I closed my eyes to sleep, all my hopes were turned down by dear slumber. So I thought about the day that passed. The convocation ceremony had got wrapped up. All my batch-mates had gathered under one roof during that day. And the best part, I had got my degree. I thought smilingly about the fest and my college. I logged on to my Facebook account to kill some more time. I floated through random people's status for a while. Unable to find anything that could interest me, I logged out.

But nothing's worse than a sleepless night followed by a really hectic day. The monsters inside my mind sought my attention and flooded it with images of a place where I had never been before. Ahmadabad. Despite the fact that I had not even been to the state where it is located, my genius-at-anticipation mind did a better job. Yes, I was happy, but sleep would make me feel better, I thought to myself.

I picked up a photo album that adorned Ishu's & my childhood. But kept it down in 20 seconds. Despite 16 years of fighting for almost every day, I realized how much I would miss him. But that's how siblings are meant to be. I glanced at my phone, to check the time. It was 2 30 am. 2:30!! I was real late for someone like me who's a die-hard admirer of slumber. But that night, I was heck sleepless.

No matter for how long I wished, I could not sleep. Not even a wink. Not even in darkness. I looked at my room, the walls. And kept looking at them. I would be thousand miles away 24 hours from now, that was all I knew. Chill ran down my spine. I got up & switched on the light. I went to see if anyone was awake. No one was, except me. That's what the switched off lights told me.

I came back and the thinking and the yawning process continued. I kept begging myself to sleep. For hours, I kept thinking, not knowing when slumber came near and cuddled me in its arms. The alarm clock gave it up at 4:30 am. Like every other morning, I could not get away giving an excuse of spending a battling night. Today, I had a flight to catch, from 200 km away from Delhi.

Leaving your home is always the worst part. No matter how much your job pays, no matter how much you have hated living in it and wanted to fly away, it always sucks. Even the fantasy and promises of the outside world fail to bring a smile on your face for a second. I wonder how strong girls are. Doing all this for a stupid.

We left the home at 5:30 in the morning. Dad wanted to drive, but I took the charge. I had always loved the feeling of driving our car, when all of us are traveling together.

On the way when Mumma was enquiring about her concerns and giving me the list of 'Do's and never Do's', dad seemed unusually quiet. I did notice but could not manage to ask about it. That's how it goes among men. Words go extinct, when they are needed the most.

We reached the airport at around 11 am. That was also the first time, I was visiting an airport. First sight at the place meant uncountable number of people biding adieu to their loved ones. Parting from each other. I wondered if the place should be actually called air-'part'. Mom & dad were with me. So, I'd to maintain the stratum of optimism & cheerfulness, at least till we were all together.

"Have you checked your ticket??" Dad asked me as we waited in the hall.

"Yes. I have."

"Good."

"So??" I wanted us to talk. I was leaving them, so I wanted to put every second in to conversation. May be dad realized that too, and that's why he was being a lil serious.

"So what??"

"Nothing. Just wanted you to know I'll take care." I told him. He smiled & nodded.

"I've asked Ishu, He would return home every evening, as his college gets over."

"Oh yes, your mom needs that too, I guess she'll need someone. I stay out a lot." He said.

"And what about you, dad??"

“Me.. I’m pretty fine. It feels nice to see your son getting fit in your shoes. But don’t get spoilt. You know what I mean.” I did. We were talking on men-on-men conditions.

“Don’t worry. I won’t. And I won’t let you down. ”

I picked my phone to call Ishu. He was the only one missing from the four of us. I wanted to talk to him casually, before I reach there.

Just as I hung up, I checked there was a new message in it, from Sirat.

It said:

"Best of luck to my fav. guitarist :)

Wish that smile always remains.

Otherwise here I’m to bring it back :)"

I replied her:

"Thanks a lot :) p.s. : I’m in roaming :P :D t.c."

I saw mum returning in 15minutes. Her fastest ever.

“I had forgotten to get these, son.” Mom said as she handled me what she had shopped. She had brought a wallet & some handkerchiefs. Both for me.

“Nothing for you.”

“I needed these only. Put your first salary, into the new one.” I stood there raising my eyebrows. So, she added “it’s lucky. Kids don’t get it.” oh ya kid, I resigned to her orders.

“Hanji, I would.”

“And call us the moment.....”

I interrupted her in between “us the moment you reach Ahmadabad & the moment you find your place. And every day twice. See mom, I have learnt it by heart.” We busted in to pangs of laughter.

The announcement was made. I had to go for check-in.

“Ohh.. Take care of yourself.” Mom said.

“I’ll, you too take care.”

"And eat properly." She reminded.

"I promise."

I looked at dad. He was smiling now. His eyes said, I'll look after your mom. They spoke even if he could not. "You also take care of yourself." I told dad.

"Yes, Papa." he replied. I smiled. My parents meant a world to me. My love could never blur for them, no matter how far I go. After the call, they embraced me and waved a goodbye. I touched their feet and came in the Checking section. They went back, for home.